THE RED STONE of the CURSES

About the Author

Mary Regan was born on a farm in County Derry but she has spent most of her life in Derry city. She lived for four years in England before returning to Derry where she now teaches in a primary school. Recently she was awarded a Master's Degree from the University of Ulster.

Her interests include folklore, archaeology and drama and she enjoys combining history with a touch of mystery. Donegal is one of her favourite places and she spends her summers in a caravan there. She is married with four children.

THE RED STONE of the CURSES

∾ MARY REGAN ∾

Book Three in the Brod of Bres Trilogy

POOLBEG

Published in 1994 by
Poolbeg Press Ltd,
Knocksedan House,
123 Baldoyle Industrial Estate,
Dublin 13, Ireland

The financial assistance of the Arts Council of Northern Ireland
is gratefully acknowledged.

A catalogue record for this book is available from the British Library.

ISBN 1 85371 432 1

Cover illustration by Jane Doran,
Cover design by Poolbeg Group Services Ltd
Set by Poolbeg Group Services Ltd in Rotis Serif 10/13.5
Printed by The Guernsey Press Ltd,
Vale, Guernsey, Channel Islands.

For Aoife

Contents

∞ It Just Couldn't be True! ∞

It was a beautiful day at the very beginning of April when the world is fresh and scrubbed clean of winter's dreary cobwebs. Aileen Kennedy was feeling very pleased with herself. All the unhappiness of the past months was behind her now and she was beginning to settle into her new life. She was actually looking forward to spending the summer on Cloughderg Mountain.

"Tom and Aggie are going into Drumenny now for the shopping, Aileen," called her mother from the open back door of the farmhouse. "Be a good girl and open the gate for them."

Aileen was gathering primroses from the mossy bank at the side of the lane. She opened the gate, stood on the bottom rung and with one foot pushed off for the free swing back to the thick hawthorn hedge. Then she propped the gate open with a stout stone and ran towards her mother.

"I think I'll go with them," she panted shoving the primroses into her mother's surprised hands.

"Do you really want to? Are you sure?"

"Yes, I'm sure," replied Aileen laughing at the startled look on her mother's face and she raced to get into the car before Tom and Aggie drove off.

Settling herself down into the back seat of the car Aileen had a good chuckle to herself. If anyone had told her six months ago that she would volunteer to go into the village with Tom Scroggy and his mother she would have told them that they were completely bonkers. How she had hated Aggie and Tom then! How furious she was when her mother, Claire Kennedy, had married Tom and brought Aileen to live in the farmhouse beneath Cloughderg Mountain!

The Scroggys were considered to be a bit odd to say the least. Tom was a farmer who had lived alone with his mother, a widow, for many years. They were both very quiet and didn't mix much. Aggie was so much a loner and her clothes so old fashioned that the local children thought she was a witch. Aileen herself had thought so at one time. At school Aileen had had to suffer a lot of vicious teasing after her mother's sudden marriage and she had loathed leaving Drumenny village to live on the Scroggy farm.

Now she felt different. Tom was a big, kind, quiet man who adored his new wife and Aggie had proved a friend to Aileen when she needed one. This would be the first time she would appear in public alone with her new step-father and his mother. It took courage to do this. Aileen knew that she would meet girls in her class who used to be her friends and that they would poke fun at her but she was ready for them now. They couldn't say anything that would really hurt her. She was proud to go round the Drumenny shops with Tom and Aggie Scroggy.

The shopping was nearly finished and Aileen thought that her luck was in and she wasn't going to meet any of her classmates. Tom and Aggie had headed back towards the car and she was just leaving the butcher's with the Sunday roast when she heard the sniggers. Nuala Deery and Lisa McCarron were lying in wait for her outside the shop.

"Well, would you look at the Alien," crowed Lisa using the nickname that Aileen hated but had grown used to. "She's out shopping with her new daddy and her Granny Scroggy!"

Aileen ignored the two girls and began to walk down the street with her head held high. They kept pace with her, one on either side.

"Did your granny buy you sweeties?"

"What's in the bag? Pigs' feet for Scroggy stew?"

"Do you get a funny smell, Nuala?" queried Lisa wrinkling up her face.

"Yeh, there's a terrible pong," nodded Nuala Deery holding her nose.

"Och it's just the good healthy dung and turf smell you get from the mountainy farmers. Do you not see the straw in her hair and the wellyboot rings on her legs?"

An angry red blush crept up Aileen's cheeks but she kept her temper in check and her mouth shut.

"Are you not talking to us?" cooed Nuala.

"She thinks she's too good for us now," decided Lisa. "She just can't wait to get back to the Scroggys, can she?"

"But she isn't a real Scroggy is she?" asked Nuala as she shook her head sadly.

"No," agreed Lisa. "Not a *really* real Scroggy. Not like the new one will be when it comes. It will be a *really* and *truly* Scroggy."

Aileen stopped dead in her tracks and swung round

on the two girls.

"Just what are you getting at?" she demanded.

"Oh, don't tell me you don't know? Sure the whole of Drumenny knows," smirked Lisa.

"Knows what?"

"That you're going to get a licklewickle baby brother or sister!"

"You're just a big liar," stammered Aileen. "A big rotten fat liar!"

The two girls burst out laughing and Aileen ran away. She stumbled blindly towards the car but a rowdy chorus followed her down the street. Lisa and Nuala were singing at the tops of their voices and just before Aileen slammed the door of the car she heard the raucous strains of "Rock-a-bye-baby".

In the kitchen Claire Scroggy was stirring pots over the stove. She turned when the door opened and beamed at her daughter.

"Did you enjoy your jaunt then?"

Aileen stared at her mother. She always wore baggy sweatshirts and loose dungarees so she looked no different than usual. Her cheeks were flushed from the heat of the stove, her black eyes sparkled and her dark glossy curls were pushed behind her ears. Aileen's heart twisted painfully. Claire looked like a happy-go-lucky teenager. She certainly didn't look old enough to have an eleven-year-old daughter.

Without answering Aileen dumped her parcel of meat on the table beside the vase of primroses and walked straight out the back door.

"What's up with her now?" she heard her mother's anxious query as she ran down the rocky path towards the beach.

4

The beach was Aileen's favourite spot in all the world. It was tucked in beneath a steep slope that rose all the way up to Cloughderg Mountain. She stood for a while gazing out over the serene waters of Lough Foyle, her long, fair hair tossing in the gentle breeze. The hair and the cornflower blue eyes were gifts from her father who had died in a motorbike accident when Aileen was a tiny baby.

It was a clear day and she could see for miles. To her right rose the rounded hump of Grianan Hill and the ancient stone fort that crowned its summit glittered in the sun. Across the Lough she could see the white frilled wakes of busy fishing boats and the jagged outlines of distant hills. She turned round and looked up. The Scroggy farm was perched precariously on a strip of level land beneath the mountain. Behind the house the cliffs soared to dizzying heights. At the very top of the mountain a huge step was gouged out as if a giant had taken a tasty nibble at the rock and at the edge of the step stood a long narrow stone pointing at the sky like an accusing finger. This left Cloughderg Mountain with a very distinctive outline.

Aileen scrambled over the shingle towards her Brooding Rock. This was a hollowed out niche that just fitted Aileen's body perfectly. Once settled there she was entirely hidden from the eyes of the world. She sat in the Brooding Rock and brooded.

It's all nonsense, she told herself. Nuala and Lisa were making it all up. They were just trying to break her temper. Yes. It was a whole big lie. Her mother would have told her, wouldn't she?

A nasty little voice nagged at the edge of her thoughts. She didn't tell you she was getting married, did she? it quizzed. And there is something different about her. She looks like a delicate flower about to bloom.

Aileen shook her head trying to clear it of worrying doubts. I'll go and see Robin, she decided jumping up. Then she remembered. It was Saturday. Since Drumenny School had discovered Robin Drake's ferocious talent on the football field he was rarely at home on a Saturday afternoon.

A stab of jealousy pierced Aileen's already troubled soul. Robin was her only friend on Cloughderg Mountain and in Drumenny School. They had grown close not only because they shared the same mountainous wilderness but because they had both been outsiders in school – Aileen because of her family situation and Robin because his father was a British soldier. His mother was a local girl but she had gone to England when she married. Robin had been brought up there. Now he was back living with his mother and grandfather in a small house below the Scroggy farm. His father was still in England and Robin missed him a lot.

Robin had shared many adventures with Aileen since he had arrived in Drumenny School in the autumn term but now she felt he was growing away from her. He too had had a terrible time with school bullies but now his popularity on the football field was protecting him. Aileen sighed and decided to go back to the house. She had nowhere else to go.

The back door was open to let in the mild spring air. There was no one in the kitchen and Aileen was just about to push open the door into the living room when she heard her name being spoken. It was Tom Scroggy who was talking and Aileen was surprised as he was a man of few words.

"I think you try to wrap Aileen up in cotton wool, Claire," she heard her stepfather say. "You can't protect her from the world all her life. I think you should tell her tonight and not put it off any longer."

"You're right, Tom. I know you are," Aileen heard her mother's muffled reply. "But she's had so much change recently and it's only within the last couple of weeks that I feel she has accepted what has happened to her. I don't want to upset her again."

"You should tell her, love. Before she hears it from somebody else."

"Oh! I've made a real mess of everything, haven't I? She just wasn't ready to hear before now. Then today when she went off to the village with you and Aggie I was so happy. I thought – she's ready now. I'll tell her when she comes back. But she had a face on her like thunder when she came in and she's away sulking again, somewhere down on the beach. Still, I *will* tell her when she comes in. I just have to, haven't I?"

"No you don't," said Aileen pushing open the door and sailing into the room. "She knows already."

"W-what do you mean?" stammered her mother.

"I know all about it. I've known for weeks. When's the big day?"

"The baby is due in the summer, probably early July," answered an amazed Claire Scroggy.

"Well isn't that grand then? You'll have something else to worry about instead of me."

Without waiting to hear a reply Aileen swept from the room and up to her bedroom.

"What do you make of that?" asked Claire.

"I don't know," replied her husband, his brow wrinkled in troubled thought.

Up in her room Aileen thumped cushions off the wall and kicked the legs of her bed.

"Well, I think you're daft!"

The words echoed round the stone walls of the old barn where Robin Drake and Aileen were taking shelter from a sudden April shower. It was Sunday morning and Aileen had just told Robin her news and what she thought about it.

"What do you mean daft?" she snapped peering at Robin's face in the dim light.

"If it was me," said Robin, "if I was getting a new brother or sister I'd be dead chuffed so I would."

"Oh you would, would you?" bristled Aileen. "Well I'm not dead chuffed. I'm dead mad! You just don't understand do you? There used to be just the two of us after my daddy died. Me and my mum. Both Kennedys. We were all right on our own. Now there'll be FOUR Scroggys and me!"

Robin stayed quiet. He knew Aileen didn't want to hear his opinion – she just wanted to let off steam.

"And she didn't even tell me," continued the distraught girl. "I had to hear it from Nuala Deery and Lisa McCarron and didn't they enjoy telling me!"

"Oh come on," cajoled Robin running out of patience. "You'll be as pleased as anybody when you get used to the idea."

"Maybe," said Aileen shrugging her shoulders. "Maybe I'll even start knitting booties."

∞ The Riddle ∞

Aileen did not get used to the idea of the new baby. As the weeks grew into months and the summer began to blossom she dreaded what July would bring. Her mother too had blossomed and the baggy sweaters no longer concealed her well-developed bump. Every time she looked at her mother Aileen felt betrayed. She was all mixed up. Besides the baby, there were other things to worry about – leaving Drumenny School for a start and then going on to the secondary school. She didn't know whether she was looking forward to the move or not; meeting new people always frightened her.

"I have here a notice about a competition for schools all over the country and I'm informing you all that Drumenny School will be represented."

Mr Quinn, the headmaster, was making his announcement to the leavers' class but his voice was so loud that probably everybody in Drumenny village heard him. The headmaster's nickname was Lambeg and it suited him perfectly. The Lambeg is a drum that is designed to be heard over great distances.

"All the leavers will participate. The entries will be judged by myself and your class teacher, Mrs McCloskey, and the winner will go forward to the

Regional Final. All the winners of the Regionals will be taken to Dublin where they will spend a weekend being entertained and then they will be presented to the President in *Áras an Uachtaráin*."

For the first time a ripple of interest stirred in the classroom. A weekend in Dublin wasn't to be sniffed at.

"The project is entitled, 'I Live Here', so you don't have to be a genius to work out that it must be a study of your own locality."

A few polite giggles greeted the headmaster's little joke.

"You may work alone or with a partner," continued Lambeg, "and the projects must be finished and mounted in the assembly hall by the 25th of June. That gives you a couple of weeks. The school library has plenty of information but the most original entry will win the prize. So I would advise you to get out there and discover something for yourselves. Look up old newspapers and talk to people – especially old people. They have great yarns to tell if anyone would listen to them."

"What on earth are we going to write about?" asked Robin as he and Aileen lay sprawled in front of the television that evening. "There's nothing on Cloughderg Mountain – but sheep and stones."

His mother, Rosaleen, giggled from the depths of her comfortable armchair but her father, Hugh Bradley, looked up from picking his lottery numbers and snorted.

"What do you mean nothing to write about in Cloughderg? Sure wasn't it once hub of the western world? High Kings passed through here and holy monks on their way to civilise the heathens of Britain and beyond. Viking hordes warred on this ground and kingdoms were lost and won!"

Robin collapsed laughing at his grandfather's mock outrage.

"Seriously, Granda," he said, "can you give us some ideas? We're really stuck."

"Well, I'd need a bit of time with my thinking cap on but I tell you what. There's a heap of old books in a tea chest in the shed. They've been in this house since ever I remember. You'll maybe find something there. There's histories and life stories, fairy tales and tall tales; any sort of tale you want. I'll hoke them out tomorrow and you can have a look through them."

"That would be great, Mr Bradley," smiled Aileen. "I'll come over after school."

"And more than welcome you are," smiled Hugh. "They may be no use to you at all but on the other hand they might give you something to think about."

True to her word, as soon as she had flung her bag under the stairs and shouted where she was going, Aileen was off to Bradley's the following afternoon.

"Come in, Aileen," called Rosaleen Drake in answer to Aileen's tap on the open door. "Robin's giving his granda a hand," she said when Aileen entered the bright kitchen. "They're over in the shed. Take a piece of cake with you."

"Thanks," said Aileen grabbing a fat triangle of sponge and rushing back out the door.

Hugh Bradley's shed was a jumble of machine parts and the tangled remains of television sets, washing machines, electric fires, smoothing irons, power drills and hair dryers. Coils of cable were heaped against the walls and gadgets with wires sprouting from them were strewn over the workbenches. Robin's grandfather was an electrical wizard and he mended anything from an egg beater to a karaoke machine. Robin was sitting in a cleared space in the middle of the floor and he was piling up books beside him as his grandfather dug them out of the tea chest.

"Just in time, Aileen," beamed Hugh. "That's the last one. You'll have your work cut out ploughing through that lot."

Aileen couldn't believe her eyes. There were books everywhere. Maybe even a hundred of them!

"Happy hunting!" laughed Hugh Bradley as he left them to their task.

There were books of every size and shape. Some were thick and heavy and some were thin and flimsy. Some were bound in dark leather and others were cloth backed and spotted with mildew. Aileen lifted one and buried her nose in it.

"I love the musty smell of them," she exclaimed.

"Some people have peculiar tastes!"

"I don't know where to begin!" said Aileen ignoring him.

"You take that pile and I'll start this one. If you find anything, shout."

The pair made themselves comfortable and they began to inspect the books. They were not very interesting. Most were very boring history books in tiny writing and had nothing to do with Cloughderg at all.

"What's that you've got?" asked Robin when he noticed that Aileen was twirling her hair – a sure sign that she was lost in a book.

"Oh . . . oh . . . nothing," replied Aileen startled out

of her reverie. "Just some old poems."

"A poetry book!" croaked Robin. "Oh that's really useful. Who're they by?"

"Somebody with a funny name."

"Well, what is it?"

"Anon."

At this Robin rolled round the floor laughing. Aileen wanted to throw the book at him. "What's so funny then?" she demanded.

At first Robin couldn't answer, then he managed to stammer between hoots, "Anon isn't a person . . . it's short for anonymous . . . that means that nobody knows who wrote them."

Aileen sat completely silent. She was mortified but she wasn't going to let Robin Drake know that.

"So, clever clogs, so you know about poems that nobody knows who wrote. Big deal!"

Robin just laughed and laughed and soon Aileen found her face cracking and she too was rolling round the floor holding her sides.

"I need to be getting home," said Aileen when she'd recovered. "I don't want to be late for dinner."

"We didn't get through very many, did we?" said Robin glancing at the still untouched books.

Aileen was looking at a small thin book that had slipped out of her pile.

"We can have another go tomorrow," she said getting to her feet. "Do you mind if I take this one home with me? I'll bring it back tomorrow."

"What is it?"

"*Magic Charms and Customs of Ancient Ireland.*"

"Trust you," sighed Robin. "Take it with you. Granda won't mind."

Aileen hated mealtimes in the farmhouse now. Generally she managed to avoid having to talk to anybody but at mealtimes she was a prisoner. There they were, all seated round the table eating Aggie's delicious lemon meringue pie. Her mother was helping herself to another slice and her pretty face was dimpled with smiles as she apologised for her greediness.

"Eat and enjoy," smiled Aggie. "Sure don't you need all you can get."

Tom was beaming his approval at his wife and Aileen just wanted to escape.

"I still have homework to finish," she said. "I'll do it in my room."

Her mother's face clouded. "You didn't finish your lemon meringue."

"I've had enough."

Once in her room Aileen curled up on her broad window-sill. It was still daylight and the summer sun had a while to go yet before it set. There wasn't a tree on the bleak hillside sturdy enough to block the breathtaking view. She could see right down the Lough to where the Foyle swept majestically towards the open ocean. Almost absentmindedly she opened the book she had brought from the Bradleys'. She read the first page.

A collection of superstitions and mystical verses gathered from the remote areas of Ireland in the year of Our Lord, 1778. Every custom, practice and magic chant noted herein was written as it was told.

Aileen began to turn the pages. They did not fire her imagination. She couldn't believe that people long ago went to such trouble to keep the fairies happy. There were stories about disgruntled little folk turning the milk sour and stealing babies, or emptying pots of precious food, bringing sickness to man and beast or cursing the churns so that no butter came.

She was nodding off when suddenly she sat up straight. The section of the book she was reading was about old riddles and on a page by itself Aileen read one that sent a shiver up her spine.

When Moon doth wax and Sun rides high
The time of reckoning is nigh.
As light doth pierce the Cursèd Stone,
When new life's bud by Death be borne,
If Two-in-One in place are twined
Keep vigil and watch as the Eye unwinds.

At the bottom of the page was a footnote explaining that the author of the book had heard the riddle from an old woman who lived in a mountainous region along the shores of Lough Foyle. She could give no meaning to the puzzle but declared she had learned it as a child at her grandmother's knee.

Most of the riddle meant absolutely nothing to Aileen but the words "Two-in-One" captured her attention. Could they be referring to the little two-faced statue – the Brod of Bres – that she had found so many months ago on the beach below her house? The little Brod had taken her into the Otherworld and the Underworld where she had had many dangerous adventures.

Now the Brod lay safely under a huge statue – the Spirit of the Foyle – that stood in the middle of the great river that flowed through Derry city. It was safe from the clutches of the Morrigan, an evil being who yearned for the power that the Brod held. The little statue had been fashioned far back before history was written when a beautiful people – the Children of the goddess Danu – had come to Ireland and had many evil forces to overcome. The Fomar lived in Ireland then. They were a base people who worshipped the wicked one-eyed god, Balor of the Evil Eye.

Bres, the King of the Danu, had a Fomar father and he betrayed his people but Lugh, the young god of light, had come to their aid. Balor and his followers were conquered and Lugh had used his magic sword to sever the head of the giant god which he then turned into stone. Bres had been punished in a similar fashion. He was turned into the little statue, the Brod of Bres. The two faces represented the two sides of his nature – the base Fomar side and the noble Danu side. Balor's head was locked forever into the mountains somewhere in Ireland. It still contained the Evil Eye.

The Children of Danu now lived happily in their Otherworld beyond the reach of human or Fomar and the Morrigan and her minions occupied the Underworld. The finding of the Brod had drawn Aileen into both worlds. The Morrigan wished to gain possession of the Brod of Bres not only for the power which the little statue itself held but because it was the key to the opening of the Evil Eye of Balor. The eye contained all the evil that the world had ever known and she wished to have the power that had once been Balor's. If that happened the Morrigan would control all the worlds and a flood of wickedness would be unleashed.

Aileen read the riddle again. She was convinced that, when solved, it would prove to be instructions for opening the one monstrous Eye of Balor. But it didn't make much sense to her – except for the last two lines. The Brod of Bres had to be placed somewhere and the Eye would open! The thought of it made her stomach churn with fear. She had seen what the Morrigan with her own Low Magic powers could do and she shuddered to think what would happen if she were successful in her quest.

The summer sun had finally dipped below the western horizon and it was growing dark. Aileen felt drowsy. She scrambled out of her clothes and slipped beneath her downy duvet. She pushed her fears to the back of her mind. Nothing could happen as long as the Brod remained locked into the base of the Spirit of the Foyle.

Before she fell asleep the last two lines of the riddle kept running through her foggy thoughts,

If Two-in-One in place are twined
Keep vigil and watch as the Eye unwinds.

∾ Meeting Old Friends ∾

"You could be right," said Robin as he studied the riddle.

"What do you mean – could be? Of course I'm right! What else could it be?" asked Aileen hotly.

"Well, it's just a load of rubbish really."

The children were again squatting on the floor of Hugh Bradley's shed surrounded by the piles of books.

"But it says the Two-in-One, that *must* be the Brod and the Eye has to be Balor's Eye!"

"Well, what if it is?" asked Robin. "We don't know what the riddle means and the Brod is under a ton of statue – and even if we had it would we *want* to find the Evil Eye? No one in their right mind would want to find that . . . except . . . "

"Except the Morrigan," interrupted Aileen.

"Yes, the Morrigan," mused Robin. "This riddle could be dangerous if it got into the wrong hands. I think we should put this book at the very bottom of the chest underneath all the other books and then forget we ever saw it."

Robin had just placed the book in the chest when he heard his mother calling from the house.

"You go on with that," he said going towards the door. "I'll be back in a minute." He ran off leaving the door swinging in the light breeze.

Hastily Aileen tore a page from her notebook and then she retrieved the book from the chest. She licked the lead of her pencil and began to copy the riddle very carefully. As she copied she read out loud. So engrossed was she in her task, and anxious to finish before Robin's return, that she didn't notice when a shadow fell across the page.

Laboriously she wrote, mouthing the words out loud as she spelled them onto the page.

Keep vigil and watch as the Eye unwinds.

She put the full stop at the last word and sat back on her heels to admire her handiwork. It was then that she noticed that the light had grown dim inside the shed. She looked towards the swinging door and her throat tightened with terror until she could barely breathe.

A grey shadow swirled in the doorway. A shadow made from the vile mists that rise from rotting graves. Aileen stared transfixed and as she stared the mist grew dense and a solid shape began to form. From out of the foul vapours came a face full of beauty and wickedness. It was a face that Aileen knew and had learned to fear – the face of the Morrigan! Yellow eyes glinted; scarlet lips curled and sneered a petrifying smile. The Morrigan threw back her head and from her long pale throat came an unearthly cry, a yowl of triumph.

The mist swirled and the shape changed. The pale throat shortened and sprouted black feathers; the slashed mouth became a gaping beak and the cry turned into the monstrous shriek of a hooded crow.

Only the yellow eyes remained unchanged. The crow stepped into the shed and then spread its black wings revealing its mist-grey body. It flew to a work bench and balanced on the very edge. Aileen could not move with fear. She clutched the sheet of paper in a trembling hand.

The bird took off again and hovered around Aileen's head, hooked talons brushing her hair and black wings beating against her face. The powerful beak stabbed at her eyes. Aileen screamed and raised her hands to protect herself. She felt the paper torn from her grasp and with a flurry of feathers and a screech of victory the ugly thief flew through the open door and out into the sunshine.

Robin was just coming across the yard when the dark shape flew out the door and they almost collided. He heard the shriek and he saw the paper jutting from the vicious beak. He feared the worst. Aileen was sitting on the floor in a state of shock. Beside her lay the open book and the notebook and pencil. Robin was quick to work out what had happened.

"But why?" he asked. "Why did you have to copy out the riddle? Didn't we decide to forget all about it?"

"No, *you* decided to forget all about it," said Aileen recovering and then she began to realise what a truly terrible thing had just happened.

"I'm sorry," she mumbled. "But I just couldn't pretend I had never seen the riddle. My brain was full of it – tumbling and turning and dying to find the answer."

"And now the Morrigan has it," sighed Robin.

Aileen sat in miserable silence.

"What should we do now?" she eventually asked in a whisper.

"I don't know. The Morrigan has the riddle but even if she does manage to find Balor's Eye she can't open it without the Brod of Bres and we know that it is safe and she can't get at it."

"Should we tell Mathgen – about the riddle, I mean?"

Mathgen was the Chief Druid of the Children of Danu and as such he was the sworn enemy of the Morrigan and the Fomar. He used his High Magic to thwart her in her efforts to gain control of the Brod and the Evil Eye. The children had first met him many months ago when Aileen had found the Brod washed up on the shore after a fierce storm. Mathgen's huge wolfhound had rescued them from the Morrigan and brought them to Killyshee Wood – the Threshold to the Otherworld and the dwelling place of the Danu. There he had told them the story of the Battle between the Danu and the Fomar and the importance of the little statue – the Brod of Bres.

"Maybe we should," nodded Robin, "even though he won't thank us for the news!"

All next day Aileen barely heard a word that was said in the classroom – even when those words were cruel and teasing. Lisa McCarron and Nuala Deery never missed an opportunity to hum the chorus of Rock-a-bye-Baby every time they passed her and half way through the morning a note appeared mysteriously on her desk.

"Have you thought of a name yet?" it said. "What about Boggy? Boggy Scroggy. Or Froggy?"

Aileen tore the note into tiny pieces and without casting a glance in the direction of the enemy she threw it in the bin. Her mind was on the riddle and the planned visit that afternoon to Mathgen's Threshold.

Impatiently the children sat in the school bus as it sped them away from Drumenny and towards Cloughderg. As soon as they got home they grabbed their bikes and after shouting something about doing work on their school project, they set off for Killyshee Wood. The weather was fine and sunny and they enjoyed the ride. Their path lay over rough bumpy ground and their mountain bikes bounced and jolted over the rocky surface. The last part of their journey was so steep and so uncomfortable that they abandoned their bikes and went on foot.

They hardly recognised the wood when they saw it nestling snugly in its lonely valley. They had seen it in the autumn when the trees were almost bare and in the spring when the tiny buds had not yet burst into leaf but now it was in its full summer dress – a canopy of speckled greenery.

Robin led the way to the rock at the heart of the wood that guarded the Threshold to the Otherworld and Aileen followed close behind.

"We're nearly there," whispered Robin. "It's a wonder the Annalaire haven't seen us."

Robin was referring to the tiny people who, although not themselves Children of Danu, belonged to the Otherworld and lived in fear of the Morrigan. They were spirits of the air but could not live long in the polluted atmosphere of the human world so they sought shelter and protection with Mathgen and the Danu. In return they guarded the entrance to the Otherworld and let no one – mortal or otherwise – come near it.

The words were hardly out of Robin's mouth when a net of the finest mesh dropped out of nowhere and captured the children in its silken folds.

"Cathara! Allochar! It's us!" shouted Aileen as she struggled to escape from the trap.

"Us?" piped a reedy voice that the children recognised as belonging to Cathara. "What's an 'Us'?"

"It looks like a monster," came the answer in a slightly deeper voice. It was Allochar, twin brother to Cathara. "A two-headed monster with four legs and four arms."

"You're just being silly now," scolded Robin in frustration as the net clung to him. "You know perfectly well who we are. Let us out!"

"Will we let the Us out?" asked Cathara mischievously. "Do you think it will attack?"

"I think it needs to learn some manners," answered her brother solemnly.

"Say, 'Please, your most clever, most beautiful, most wonderful highnesses, please set us free!'"

Robin coughed and spluttered and muttered and the net closed tighter until the children were almost strangled.

"All right!" gasped Aileen. "Please, Your most Clever, Most beautiful, Most Wonderful Highnesses, *please* set us free!"

The net miraculously dropped away and Robin and Aileen were free. They were surrounded by grinning faces. Every branch of every tree was draped with Annalaire and just above their heads stood Cathara and Allochar. Their smiles were as wide as the mouth of the Foyle. The bad temper melted away and the children laughed in delight to see their old friends again.

23

The twins were slightly shorter than either Robin or Aileen but they were fully grown adults. Red-gold hair drifted about their shoulders and fringed the chin of Allochar. He wore a tunic of pale leather and leggings of woven thistledown. His sister was dressed in a gossamer gown the colour of wild bluebells and her legs and feet were bare. Each twin wore a pouched leather belt that crossed at the shoulders and buckled at the waist. As the children had already discovered, these pouches held many interesting secrets.

From many tiny fingers, dainty threads were spun and the Annalaire swung, like trapeze artists, from their lofty perches and soon surrounded Aileen and Robin.

"What brings you here?" asked Cathara as she formally shook Aileen's hand. The purple irises of her huge eyes had narrowed in anxiety. "I trust it is not bad tidings?"

"You know you should not come to the Wood unless extreme danger looms," added Allochar tugging at his downy beard. "It is not difficult to rouse Mathgen to a terrible anger."

The children exchanged furtive glances and then Aileen coughed nervously. It was she who had allowed the Morrigan to steal the Riddle so she felt obliged to do the talking.

"We must see Mathgen," she announced.

"Impossible!" stormed Allochar. "At this season it is impossible! Don't you know that, child?"

"W . . . w . . . what do you mean?" stammered Aileen.

"This a very busy time for the Children of Danu. They are approaching the Great Festival of Light when their mother, the goddess Danu, invites them to visit their old homeland again. The preparations are under way and nothing must disturb them. Mathgen will not be called across the Threshold."

"You must try!" urged Robin. "We are your friends. You *must* try. It is important."

Cathara and Allochar went into a huddle to discuss the situation and the children waited anxiously for their reply.

"You ask much of us," announced Allochar, "but friendship binds us closely. We will summon Mathgen but I fear he will not answer."

The twins led them towards the very heart of the wood and soon they were standing at the great rock, the Threshold of the Otherworld. The Annalaire surrounded the rock and held hands tightly. A low chant began that soon soared to a high singing whine. Beads of sweat broke out on Annalaire brows and their faces grew so pale with the strain that Aileen was sure she could see right through their delicate, translucent skin. On and on they chanted but Mathgen did not materialise. In vain the children looked for his flowing white hair and beard and his white rod of High Magic.

At last the circle broke as Annalaire began to collapse in exhaustion on the forest floor.

"It is useless," panted Cathara breathlessly. "Mathgen is beyond any call from this world."

"Then we must go to his!" announced Aileen firmly.

A babble of nervous talk broke out among the excited people.

"You must take us with you when you return."

Even Robin was surprised at Aileen's insistence.

"Return we must, and immediately, for we are worn out," replied Allochar. "But if we brought mortals beyond the Threshold then Mathgen's anger would know no bounds. He would banish us from the Otherworld and we would soon perish on this mortal earth."

"If we do not see Mathgen there may be no worlds left for any of us. Only the Underworld will survive if the Morrigan opens the Evil Eye of Balor!"

Shocked silence greeted Aileen's dramatic declaration. Then a quiver of fear rippled through the Annalaire.

"You have spoken the name of all the Evils!" whispered Cathara. "A name that we have not uttered since Lugh chopped off his head and turned it into stone."

"Well, it needs to be spoken now. We have a warning for Mathgen and we must deliver it."

Again Allochar went into a huddle with his sister.

"You have always spoken the truth to us in the past and so we must trust you now," he announced sadly when he returned. "We will take you with us across the Threshold and into the Otherworld. But we are risking our very existence. If this is a trick then the Annalaire will be no more!"

"What have you got us into now!" moaned Robin.

∽ The Otherworld ∽

"To cross to the Otherworld you must obey our every word. Hold hands tightly and neither cry out nor speak until you have been given permission to do so."

"Will we get back all right?" Aileen asked, suddenly getting cold feet.

"If you can persuade Mathgen that your visit is necessary then he will allow you to return to your own world and he will not punish us," replied Allochar looking her straight in the eye. "Once you are in Mathgen's presence you hold all our lives in your hands."

Aileen swallowed hard; then she looked at Robin with a question in her eyes.

"I always like seeing new places," he said with a grin and Aileen was glad she had him for a friend. He was game for anything.

"Right," she said grinning back at him, "give me your hand." Then she added with a giggle as she grasped his outstretched hand, "If they could see us now in Drumenny School!"

As soon as Aileen and Robin clasped hands their bodies felt strangely light as if they were on the point of floating off into space. They began to twirl, gently at first and then faster and faster until they were in the epicentre of a whirlwind that caught them up and carried them off towards a distant pinpoint of light. The force was so powerful that Aileen wanted to cry out but she bit her lip and held more tightly onto Robin's hand.

Suddenly they were on firm ground again. It was the same ground they had been on before but the huge stone was no longer there. In its place stood a massive iron gate that stretched high up into the tree canopy that now arched miles above their heads. It was the same place and yet it was not. Something had changed. Robin and Aileen knew that they had travelled into a time and place that was strange and unknown to them. Allochar, Cathara and all the Annalaire were still with them but their positions were reversed. The twins now towered over the children!

Silently the twins stepped up to the gate and put the palms of their hands flat against the ornate bars. Then they closed their eyes tightly and their hands began to glow. The gate began to open. Slowly, and with many creaks of protest, the huge gate swung back. The twins stepped across the Threshold and they beckoned the children to follow them.

Once through the gate the children knew that they had finally crossed into a different world. It was a bright world – a world filled with sunshine but without shadows. A dazed Aileen and Robin found themselves on a rolling plain of lush, green grass on which grazed herds of plump cattle. A sky-blue lake filled a dip in the plain and in the middle of it, floating magically on the water, was a building as large as a cathedral. It had a steeply pitched roof of pale yellow metal and walls white as a snow drift. A pathway of stepping-stones lay across the lake and the twins led them towards it.

Soon they were walking through an avenue flanked by trees bearing strange fruits and exotic blooms. Large, richly coloured butterflies flitted from one bright flower to another and the air was filled with birdsong. They stood now before a stout timber door that opened to the finger touch of Cathara.

At first it was dark in the vast inner hall but, as their eyes grew accustomed to the gloom, the children could see tall figures sitting in groups around the room. A loud buzz of conversation, music and laughter echoed off the walls and there was a delicious smell of cooking.

Slowly silence descended as all eyes swivelled towards the intruders. The children felt very uncomfortable. Either they were in the company of a giant race of people or the journey had shrunk *them* to midget size. They did not like being so small.

The giants were all women, as far as they could see, and they had been engaged in a variety of activities before being interrupted. Some had been playing board games, others were gathered round a harp and some were sewing. They did not seem annoyed at the intrusion, merely curious, but it was this curiosity that brought home to the children that they were outsiders in a strange world and here without invitation.

The women were all young and very beautiful. There wasn't a dark head among them and each fair head was braided and encircled with a band of gold. All were similarly dressed in calf-length tunics and cloaks but the colours were bright and many. Green, blue and deep purple cloaks, pinned with gold or silver brooches, covered tunics edged with swirling patterns of bright embroidery. Twists of gold coiled round elegant wrists and gold again adorned pale throats. The softly draping tunics were gathered at the waist with woven belts of rainbow-coloured threads.

Allochar and Cathara marched Aileen and Robin through the ranks of staring women towards a high throne-like chair. Groups of musicians were seated round the chair and in it sat the most magnificent creature the children had ever seen.

At a respectful distance from the throne the twins bowed so low that their heads almost touched the ground and indicated that the children should do likewise. Aileen and Robin felt a bit silly but they bowed to the lovely woman seated before them. She was dressed much as the other women but everything about her was richer and more ornate. Her red cloak, the only one of that colour in the hall, was edged in gold-threaded embroidery of the most intricate designs. Her blue-white tunic shone with the lustre of pure silk and was clasped at the waist by a belt of precious metals and stones. Gold glittered at her neck and wrists and on her head sat a jewel-encrusted circlet of red gold. The brooch pinning her cloak was as big as a plate and the designs in gold and silver matched the swirls on her cloak.

"Who have you brought here, Spirits of the Air, and at whose instruction?"

The voice was as beautiful as the woman but it was neither welcoming nor friendly. At her words the twins straightened up and the children did the same.

"We have brought two mortal children to the Dun of Scothniamh, O Queen," replied Allochar. "They are acquainted with the Druid, Mathgen, and have news of

30

grave importance for him."

"What news can this be that you have broken the Law of the Otherworld and brought mortals here without permission?"

"It concerns the goddess of war and destruction, O Queen – the Morrigan herself," spoke Cathara.

"And the Fomar god, Balor of the Evil Eye," added Allochar.

At their words the Queen's strong hands gripped the golden arms of her chair but her expression did not change.

"Speak, mortals," she commanded. "I, Scothniamh, Queen of this Dun, demand that you tell of the doings of the Morrigan."

Aileen looked towards the twins. She remembered the warning about not speaking without permission. The twins nodded impatiently.

"Well," began Aileen hesitantly, "it is a very long story."

"We are very fond of stories," replied Queen Scothniamh and the other women began to gather round the throne. "It all began when I first found the Brod of Bres."

A ripple of concern greeted Aileen's first words.

"The Morrigan took it from me and she nearly managed to steal for herself the power of the Brod."

A startled gasp exploded on the air.

"But we stopped her! Me and Robin and the Annalaire and Mathgen."

A sigh of relief whispered round the room.

"But she nearly got her hands on it again."

There was another communal intake of breath.

"The Brod was under Grianan Fort with the Warriors

of Danu but the hill caved in and the Brod was found. It was put into the museum in Derry and one of her servants stole it."

Little squeals of fear and a flurry of hands covering mouths greeted this development.

"But we got it back again and now it is safe under a big statue in the middle of the River Foyle!"

The tension in the room relaxed and the women sat back on their heels.

"You tell a good story, for a mortal child," sighed the Queen settling back from the edge of her throne. Then a puzzled frown creased her lovely brow.

"If the Brod of Bres is safe from the greedy grasp of the Morrigan, why have you come here? What do you want with Mathgen?"

"Well, that's another part of the story," whispered Aileen and her voice seemed to wither and dry up.

"We found something else, you see," said Robin coming to her rescue.

"Yes?" The Queen raised a quizzical eyebrow.

"It was in an old book. It's a very old Riddle."

"We love riddles as much as stories," smiled the Queen.

"We think it tells how to find the Eye of Balor and how to open it."

If Robin had let loose a wild tiger in the hall it couldn't have had more effect! There were squeals and cries, huggings and moanings, tears and tantrums before Queen Scothniamh clapped her hands and called for silence.

"What you say is impossible!" she said sternly, glaring at the frightened children. "Lugh, the young god of the sun, destroyed Balor and his Evil Eye. It will

32

never be found again!"

"I think you're wrong," said Robin quietly but firmly. "Whoever solves the Riddle will find the Eye. And . . . "

"And," interrupted Aileen feeling she had to confess her guilt, "the Morrigan has the Riddle!"

This time the reaction round the room was of stunned disbelief.

"Send for my Druid," announced the Queen and her voice had gone low and ponderous. "Tell Mathgen I have need of him."

Two of the women went towards a door behind the throne and Scothniamh now beamed a radiant smile at the children.

"We must show our guests hospitality," she said. "Even if they come without bidding and bearing dark tidings."

At that the harp music started up and a feather cushion as big as a mattress was placed on the floor for Aileen and Robin to sit on. A footstool served as a table and on it was placed a silver plate filled from a steaming cauldron. Fragments were broken from large flat cakes of bread and the children were encouraged to dunk them in the aromatic stew.

A ravenous hunger overwhelmed them and soon they were lapping up the delicious juices and picking out pieces of tender meat with their fingers. The ladies took silver thimbles from their fingers and filled two of them with water and two with a dark gold liquid. The children dipped their fingers in the water and drank the golden liquid. It tasted of long summer days and fragrant wild blossoms.

They were right in the middle of their meal when

Mathgen came through the door followed by Cuan, his hound. At first they did not recognise the Druid. He too was giant sized but he was also years younger. He no longer stooped and his face was smooth and free from wrinkles. His flowing white beard and mane of hair were now fiery red and his step was jaunty and full of energy. It wasn't until he spoke that the children were certain that it was indeed Mathgen.

"My Lady Scothniamh," came the familiar voice as the Druid bowed to the Queen, "you summoned me to your presence."

The Queen merely nodded in the direction of the children. Mathgen turned round and when he saw the children his expression was one of shock.

"Aileen the Fair and Robin of the Questions!" he cried using the names he had given them when they had first met. Then his shock turned to anger. He whirled on the Annalaire.

"You have disobeyed my orders, you imps of the air!" he stormed at Allochar and Cathara. "You have brought mortals across the Threshold! You know well your punishment. Henceforth you are banished from the Otherworld. The Gates of the Threshold will no longer respond to your chants and charms!"

The twins fell to their knees and prostrated themselves before Scothniamh and Mathgen.

"My Lord Mathgen . . . " began Allochar.

"Silence!" roared Mathgen and his powerful voice rolled round the cavernous reaches of the room.

"Don't speak to him like that!"

Every eye in the room was staring at the tiny mortal who dared to scold Mathgen the Druid.

"They were only trying to help us – *and* the Children

of Danu. It isn't their fault. They didn't want to bring us here; it was all my idea. So if you have to blow your top then blow it at me!"

Stunned silence greeted Aileen's outburst. Then Queen Scothniamh began to laugh softly.

"Even I, Queen of a Royal Dun, would quail before the anger of a Wizard of the High Magic," she laughed. "This mortal child has courage. We will hear what she has to say about the Morrigan and this Riddle."

She turned then to the prostrate figures and said, "Arise Children of the Annalaire and pray to the gods that these mortals can save you from exile. Recite the Riddle," she commanded.

Aileen cleared her throat and began.

When Moon doth Wax and Sun rides high
The time of reckoning is nigh.
As light doth pierce the Cursèd Stone
When new life's bud by Death be borne
If Two-in-One in place are twined
Keep vigil and watch as the Eye unwinds.

When Aileen had finished she told of the copying of the mysterious words and the Morrigan's mocking laughter as she flew off with her stolen goods. As she spoke fear seemed to creep round the edges of the room and into every heart. Even Mathgen forgot his anger and listened intently. When she had finished the Druid began to pace the floor, tugging at his beard and repeating the Riddle to himself over and over again. No one dared interrupt his ruminations.

It was a revelation to the children to see how deeply Mathgen was respected and even feared in the

Otherworld. Here in his own world, Mathgen was a different person. He was no longer the peculiar, fumbling old man that the children had known, but a powerful figure who commanded obedience. But perhaps because the children had seen him in *their* world they did not stand in awe of him.

At last Mathgen's pacing came to a stop.

"What does your great knowledge make of the strange Riddle, Mathgen of the Power?" queried the Queen anxiously.

"It is a Riddle conjured up by a Magician of the highest order, My Lady," replied the Druid. "It is a Riddle not meant to be easily solved."

"Do you think the Morrigan can solve it?"

Mathgen straightened to his full imposing height indicating his annoyance at the suggestion that the Morrigan's powers might be greater than his own.

"It is a long time since Balor ruled and much knowledge has been lost, My Lady – to the Fomar as well as to the Danu. We do not know where lies the ugly head and how the Eye will be opened. This Riddle will have to be given time – but, have no fear, the Morrigan will not solve it before Mathgen."

"I'm glad to hear it," said the Queen. "Can you tell us nothing of the meaning?'

"When the Moon doth wax and the Sun rides high," quoted Mathgen dreamily; "now that is a puzzle. The Powers of Light are strongest when the sun is high and the Powers of Darkness are at their height when the moon is full. The sun is at its zenith at midday and for the moon to wax full at the same time is an impossibility. Where the Cursed Stone lies I know not, and what is to be borne away by Death I cannot fathom. But, be assured, no harm can come to us at this time. I will reveal the mystery of the Riddle before danger looms."

Mathgen rushed through this speech as if he knew quite well that he was not exactly dazzling the company with his great powers of detection and then he slowed down to give importance to his next statement.

"The Two-in-One is of course the Brod of Bres – the statue made in the image of our treacherous ancestor, King Bres. Without it the Evil Eye cannot be opened and, My Lady, I have taken care that the Brod is safe and cannot be used for the Morrigan's evil designs."

Aileen looked at Robin and the two nearly burst out laughing. They had been there when the Brod had been imprisoned in its present resting place. It had happened by accident – an accident caused by Mathgen's careless fumbling!

"Will this endanger our preparations for the Great Festival of Light and our journey to Inisfail, our ancient Homeland?" asked Queen Scothniamh.

"Do not furrow your brow with worry, My Lady Scothniamh," smiled the Druid. "The Morrigan will not solve the Riddle before Mathgen. Her powers are weak at this time. If she is ever to challenge the Children of Danu it will be at Samhain, the dark time when evil is strong and wanders freely. We are at the half circle of the sun's journey and Samhain is far away. Now it is the time of the Children of Danu; the time when the sun is in the ascendancy and the days are filled with light. My High Magic is at its most powerful. We need not fear the Morrigan. We can make our joyous journey in peace."

"We must make ready then," decided the Queen happily. "I will leave all matters concerning the Morrigan and the Riddle in your capable hands, Mathgen. Are the warriors ready to travel with us aboard the Great Sea-God's ship?"

"Their swords and spears are at the ready," assured Mathgen, "and they practise endlessly for the Games. The Poets have been busy too and you will hear much that will please you."

"My maidens will run as fast as any warrior and throw a spear as far as the night stars," laughed Scothniamh. "We will give the men good sport. And we have songs that will drown the dreary drone of their Poets. Now we must bid farewell to the mortal children. You, Mathgen, will accompany them to the Threshold."

As the children and the Annalaire followed Mathgen out of the great house and over the grassy plain the women of the Dun gathered at the door to wave farewell.

"You did well to bring me this Riddle," said Mathgen when they reached the great iron gates, "but now I think you must leave it with me and look no more for the dark side of the Otherworld. If I cannot solve the Riddle in the whisper of a breath then the Morrigan will not solve it in a thousand times a thousand years."

Mathgen now bent down and placed his hands on the heads of the children. Away from the Royal Court his anger had vanished and he was more like the old Mathgen that they knew and loved. They could see kindness and concern in his eyes.

"The Morrigan is an ugly woman, my children," he

said softly, "and she likes to use Mortals in her evil plans. You are therefore in great danger if you seek her out. Many times she has tried to trick the Children of Danu into war with the Fomar so that she can feast on the blood of the battlefield. This is another of her wily tricks. She cannot solve the Riddle but she knew you would come to me with it. She is waiting in her Pit of the Hell Hag hoping that we will attack but the Children of Danu are not fools. She can fester in her hell-hole while we enjoy ourselves with our Mother Danu, in Inisfail."

Mathgen then commanded the Annalaire to see the children safely over the Threshold and back to their own world.

"We are indebted to you," said Cathara when they once again stood in Killyshee Wood. "You saved us from the wrath of Mathgen. We must return a favour with a favour. Is there anything you wish us to do for you?"

If ever you are asked a question like that you cannot think of a single thing to ask for. Aileen thought for a while and then she shrugged her shoulders.

"Can I save the favour for when I know what I want?"

"You can call on us at any time," replied Cathara. "Whenever you need our help you have only to wish for it."

As Robin and Aileen walked back towards their hidden bikes they talked about the happenings in the Dun of Scothniamh.

"Do you feel any better?" queried Aileen. "I mean Mathgen seems certain he will solve the Riddle before the Morrigan and that there can be no trouble from her now. He was very confident."

"He always is," replied Robin.

"He is right about one thing." said Aileen. "The Morrigan can't do anything without the Brod of Bres and she certainly cannot lay her sticky claws on that!"

∽ Cloch Dearg ∽

"So, I suppose it's back to the books then," said Aileen grumpily. A week had passed since the discovery of the Riddle and the pair had not been able to settle themselves to do anything about their school project. They hadn't even decided on a title and they were running out of time. The weather was beautiful and it was too hot to think about work. They were lying on the grass soaking up the sun on a Friday afternoon and, after a day at school, they didn't feel like moving.

"We'll start tomorrow," said Robin yawning.

They would, too, thought Aileen. It was great to have Robin back again on Saturdays now that the football season was over.

"Humph!" came a loud snort from behind Hugh Bradley's newspaper. Robin's grandfather was sitting in an armchair in the doorway of the house enjoying the warmth of the afternoon.

"What's up with you now, Dad?" asked Robin's mother as she scattered corn to their four hens.

Her father rattled the newspaper impatiently.

"Workmen nowadays," he said sticking his head out from behind the paper, "they're fit for nothing."

"What do you mean?"

"They couldn't build mud pies in a bog!"

"Are you talking about all workmen everywhere or is there somebody in particular annoying you?" smiled his daughter as she leaned over him to get a look at the paper.

"Could you credit it? All the ballyhoo and razzmatazz there was about the oul' thing when they put it up on St Patrick's Day and there it is falling down already!"

"What's falling down, Dad? What are you talking about?"

"Have you no eyes in your head at all, girl? There," said Hugh stabbing the paper with his finger, "that gazebo of a statue they put up in the middle of the Foyle, there's cracks in the base of it as wide as Shipquay Gate!"

"Do you mean the Spirit of the Foyle, Granda?" asked Robin stopping dead in the middle of a yawn.

"Aye, that's the fancy name they gave it. Well, the Spirit is no longer at her best. They say she's a danger to river traffic and they're building a cage of scaffolding around her!"

Hugh went on grumbling to himself and his daughter Rosaleen left him to it. Aileen and Robin looked at each other in horror.

"If there's a crack at all, I bet the Morrigan knows about it," whispered Robin.

"I'll bet you 5p to a fiver that she not only knows about it but she has the Brod already!"

"Come on over to the shed," answered Robin. "We need to think about this."

Once in the privacy of the shed Robin and Aileen soon lost their summer laziness.

"She has the Riddle and now she has the Brod,"

announced Aileen as she paced the floor. "I just know it! You know the way she can change shape. She could turn herself into a worm or a diving bird or anything and it would be no bother to her to crawl into a crack. She lives in one!"

"And she has plenty of creepie-crawlie friends; any one of them could have told her about the cracks," agreed Robin.

"Well, what do we do now?" asked Aileen.

"Mathgen says she can't possibly solve the Riddle."

"Sometimes Mathgen would talk through his hat if he had one," said Aileen flatly.

"What do you mean?"

"Well, he wasn't exactly terrific when he was trying to solve the Riddle himself, was he?"

"Do you think we should try to tell him about the cracks in the statue?" asked Robin.

"I think the whole lot of them are probably away on their summer holidays to this Inisfail place and are more interested in who wins the races than what the Morrigan is doing," decided Aileen. Then a great big beam of a smile lit her face.

"I've just had a brill idea!" she announced. "Our project! It's sitting looking at us in the face!"

"Project?" queried Robin, puzzled by the switch in the conversation

"You heard Lambeg," gushed Aileen warming to her subject. "He said, 'Be original'. Suppose we solve the Riddle and suppose we prove that the old Legend of Balor's eye is not only true but that the Eye itself is here in Cloughderg; well, you can't get more original than that can you?"

"You're doing a lot of supposing there," said Robin

doubtfully. "What makes you think the Eye is here in Cloughderg? It could be anywhere in Ireland."

"But the Riddle was told by an old woman living in the mountains on the banks of Lough Foyle, fat head!" said Aileen irritably. "Not, 'anywhere in Ireland!'"

"Where would we start?" asked Robin throwing in the towel.

"I think the Riddle *tells* us the 'How, Where and When' of the opening of the Eye. We should start with the 'Where'," said Aileen decisively.

"What does the Riddle tell us about the 'Where'?"

"The only thing in the Riddle that seems to be real – a real solid thing I mean – is the Cursèd Stone," and Aileen softly quoted from the Riddle,

"As light doth pierce the Cursed Stone."

"If the stone *is* around here," said Robin, "I don't know anything about it. I haven't lived here long enough."

"Neither have I," sighed Aileen. Then her eye fell on the box of books.

"As I said before," she said pointing to them, "it's back to the books."

They were nearly an hour scrutinising the books before they struck gold. It was Robin who found the musty old leather-bound book with tissue-paper-thin pages and tiny writing. It was the title that caught his eye.

"I think we might find something here," he shouted in excitement.

"What is it?"

"It's called *What's in a Name?* and it seems to give the stories behind all the place-names around Lough Foyle."

"Is there anything about Cloughderg?" squeaked Aileen almost tearing the book from Robin's grasp.

"Hold your horses!" commanded Robin. "I'll find out in a minute."

Aileen could hardly contain herself while Robin calmly ran his finger down the contents page and then grunted in satisfaction.

"Page forty-three!" he announced.

Under the entry for Cloughderg they found exactly what they were looking for and this is what they read:

"CLOUGHDERG: From the Irish, *Cloch Dhearg* (Red Stone). This is a modern, shortened form and the more ancient name can be found on old maps (see p.118). The older name, Cloch Dhearg na Mallachtaí, means the Red Stone of the Curses. The origin of the name is obscure but older people in the area believe it is connected with the legend of the Dagda's son.

The Dagda was the chief god of the mythical people the Tuatha de Danaan who claimed the Dagda's wife, Danu, as their mother. According to the legend, one Corgenn killed the Dagda's son and his punishment was to carry the body on his back until he found a stone the exact length and breadth of the dead body. This he found on the shores of Lough Foyle and there he buried the Dagda's son and raised the stone over him. The hill was called the Hill of Sighs and the Dagda wept tears of blood over his son and cursed the place forever. Thus the name – the Red Stone of the Curses."

Eagerly the children turned to page 118 and there they found a folded map of the Cloughderg area. The writing on the map was tiny and some of the spelling peculiar but they found it – the Red Stone of the Curses. It was right at the top of Cloughderg Mountain!

"That must be the stone that stands up like a finger," breathed Aileen. "Right above the Scroggy house!"

"Have you ever been up there?" asked Robin.

Aileen shook her head.

"I don't know if anyone's ever been up there. It would be impossible to climb those cliffs – especially in winter."

"But look!" exclaimed Robin. "There is a footpath marked on the map. It's round the other side of the mountain where the slope is more gentle."

"The map is hundreds of years old," replied Aileen twirling her hair. "There's probably no path there now."

"Tomorrow's Saturday," said Robin. "How do you fancy going for a long hike and a picnic? You'd never know what we'd find."

∽ Creatures of the Depths ∽

On Saturday the good weather had broken. It was very overcast and the conditions were not ideal for hiking.

"Can't you put it off till another day," suggested Aileen's mother, "when it might be a bit more promising?"

"That could be never," answered Aileen. "It's probably as good today as it's going to be all summer."

"Where do you plan to go?" asked Aggie Scroggy looking up from the baking bowl in which she was mixing a huge scone of bread.

"We're just poking around looking for something to write our project on," said Aileen but she didn't look the old woman in the eye. Aggie had an uncanny way of knowing what was going on in Aileen's mind.

"Well, I don't like you wandering about and me not knowing where you are," said her mother anxiously.

"Ach, they'll be all right," smiled Tom Scroggy pulling on his boots before heading to the fields. "You fuss a bit, Claire. She's a big girl now. Sure what harm can they get up to around here? I was a great one myself for the exploring."

Aileen stared at her step-father in astonishment; it was the longest speech she had ever heard him make! But she was grateful for his blessing. So, after her mother had checked for warm clothes and stout shoes, Aileen prepared to escape.

"If you go anywhere near the mountain," whispered Aggie as Aileen passed the table on the way to the door, "be careful. It can be dangerous – even in summer."

Although Cloughderg Mountain rose straight up behind the Scroggy house, the children turned their backs on it and set off in the opposite direction. Robin was well equipped for the journey. He had a good orienteering compass, a small camping stove and a knife with a dozen different blades. He had all sorts of gadgets for outdoor living that had belonged to his father and they were neatly packed into a very good rucksack. Aileen had brought sausages and a loaf of bread in a plastic bag. She was a bit ashamed of herself when she saw how well Robin had prepared for the trip. He had one item he was specially proud of. After Aileen had gone home the previous evening, he had shown the map in the book to his grandfather and the two of them had made an enlarged copy of it onto a sheet of drawing paper. It was now covered in polythene and folded neatly in the rucksack.

They had decided not to take their bikes as the search for the footpath would have to be done on foot. The sky was broody with black clouds as they began their trek. They left the lane through the first gap in the hedge and as soon as they were out of sight of the house they sat down to study the map.

"The footpath should begin here somewhere but there is no sign of it," said Robin pacing up and down the rocky hillside.

"Well, can't we just go in the same general direction

and keep an eye out for landmarks? Look," exclaimed Aileen poking the map with her finger, "there's a lake or something. The path goes right round it. We're bound to find that. What's that written beside it?"

"Lough Shule," replied Robin. "My granda says it means the Weird Lake." Then he pulled out his compass. "We'd need to walk in a northerly direction."

It took them nearly an hour to cover the rough ground that climbed gently but steadily to the base of the mountain. They could see no sign of a lake. Ahead of them lay two low hills with a dip in the middle.

"I think that's a path going to that wee valley," said Aileen squinting up her eyes.

"Maybe," replied Robin, "but it's more likely that it's just animal tracks."

Aileen looked at the long thin ribbon of water on the map.

"Well, if there's a lake at all, it should be in that valley so I think we should follow the track," she decided.

"There may have been a lake called Lough Shule in the sixteen hundreds or whenever the map was drawn," wheezed Robin sitting down to rest on a rock, "but it's either dried up now or gone underground."

"Maybe it's up at the head of the valley," suggested Aileen. "If we go a bit further in we might find it."

That was easier said than done. The floor of the valley was a mini-jungle of young pussy willow trees and it was impossible for the children to see where they were going.

"The valley runs exactly north-south," said Robin studying the compass, "so if we keep going north we will either find the lake or come to the head of the valley."

The further into the valley they went the wetter the ground got and reeds grew tall and spiky.

"That's a good sign," said Aileen. "We must be getting close to water."

She had no sooner uttered the words than they had emerged from the reed bed and were splashing in peaty lake shallows. The stones beneath their feet were visible in the coffee-coloured liquid but one step further on and the lake bed slid away into a deep, dark mystery. The lake stretched black and empty in the bleak landscape. No wild waterfowl cruised the lonely waters; no birdsong interrupted the silence.

"Lough Shule – the Weird Lake!" whispered Aileen, afraid to disturb the brooding solitude of the watery wilderness.

Suddenly there was a great boiling rumble in the centre of the lake and the water began to spume and spout in frothy temper. As if from a cesspool of demons, a primeval head heaved and towered above the children, terrifying them with its size and its gaping mouth. It was the head of a gigantic eel with eyes like shards of ice and two regimented rows of razor teeth in a hungry mouth. Behind the monstrous head the blue-grey body rippled in humps of coiled, ferocious energy.

"Run!" shouted Robin as the ugly beast-head swayed towards them.

It was impossible to run through the reeds and the forest of young willows. As Robin and Aileen pushed aside the supple branches they seemed to come alive and lash back at them with painful stinging thwacks. Behind them they could hear the thrashing of the giant eel as it sought an unexpected meal.

"Keep going!" panted Robin as he urged Aileen forward.

Aileen tried to keep going but above her a dark shadow loomed. The great head came crashing out of the sky flattening yards of willows in its wake and Aileen found herself looking straight into the cold, cruel eyes. Slime from the sticky body drenched her clothes and she could feel the warmth of fetid breath and smell the stench of rotten fish.

At first the beast seemed just as startled as Aileen and it hesitated for a few moments before going in for the attack. Aileen used those precious moments to look around for Robin. She couldn't find him! Where was he? Then she saw him. He was hacking at a willow rod with his pocket knife.

"What are you doing?" she shouted as she tried to squirm away from the ravenous jaws. The eel lifted its bullet-shaped head and stayed poised over her trembling body as if savouring her terror. Then it tired of the game. It was time for dinner. Slowly the head descended and the slit mouth parted. Aileen closed her eyes and tensed herself for the attack.

An ear-splitting yell turned the next few minutes into a chaotic nightmare. Aileen recognised Robin's voice and then she saw a flash of his blue tracksuit as he pushed her roughly out of the way. Right up to the beast he rushed, yelling as he ran. Then he raised his arm and plunged the pointed willow rod right into the steely eye of the monster.

The giant eel screamed in pain and the ugly head twisted and turned in a desperate effort to dislodge the searing splinter. Clots of black blood spurted from the eye and showered over the children. The air was rent with howls of raging agony and then, amid roars and rumbles, crashings and thrashings, the eel began to writhe its way back to the cool dark waters of the lake.

Once free from the threat of the eel and the punishing grip of the willows, Robin and Aileen flung themselves down on the ground in total exhaustion.

"Now we know why it was called the Weird Lake," panted Aileen.

"You know what?" said Robin. "I'm starving with hunger. I could just murder those sausages." Aileen stared at him in disbelief.

"How can you think of food now? You're disgusting. Even thinking about sausages is making my stomach turn." But Aileen was wrong. The tempting smell of the sausages as they sizzled on the frying pan got to her and soon she was tucking into a dripping sausage sandwich.

"Now," said Robin as they cleared up after themselves, "we go that way to get to Cloughderg Mountain."

"You still want to go after what's happened?" asked Aileen.

"We have to. If the Morrigan has solved the Riddle and she has the Brod then there may be no time to lose. She could open Balor's Eye at any moment and God help us all then!"

"You're right," agreed Aileen. "We have to stop her! The Eye must be up there near the Cursed Stone. If we find that we have solved part of the Riddle at least."

From now on the ground began to rise more steeply and soon the children realised they were on the lower slopes of the mountain. It looked different from this angle and they could see neither the summit nor the standing stone pointing at the sky. It did not look like one mountain at all but a rolling series of humped crags.

"That seems to be a path," said Aileen pointing to a trail through the heather made by wandering sheep.

"Yes," said Robin. "It looks easy enough from here but God knows what it's like further up."

Up they went like sheep one after the other, as the path was narrow. The going was fairly easy at first but then it began to drizzle and the ground became slippery. Boulders, dripping streamlets of water, blocked their view so that they were never sure they were climbing in a straight line.

After climbing for about an hour they were surprised to find the ground levelling out again and disappointed to see that they still had a long way to go. The rain had stopped and they had grown very warm during the climb so they had stripped to their tee-shirts. Now suddenly, it became very chilly and they pulled on their tracksuit tops again. Thick clouds drooped over the mountainside and began to curl round their heads. It was a cold fog that shimmered with a frost-blue light. Soon they could not see their feet at all and rocks loomed menacingly out of the eerie mist as if trying to block their path.

They were stumbling around in circles and the compass was no help to them at all. The needle was swinging wildly in all directions. When they passed the same rock three times they knew they were hopelessly lost. They tried to keep going and Robin threw pebbles ahead of their feet to make sure they were walking on firm ground. Suddenly there was no reassuring rattle.

"Stop!" he commanded and got down on his hands

and knees. Slowly he inched forward, feeling the ground with his fingers. They met fresh air! The children were on the edge of a precipice!

"What are we going to do?" asked Aileen in a frightened voice.

"We'd better wait until the mist lifts," decided Robin trying to sound brave. They sat on a rock and huddled together for warmth and comfort.

"Listen!" whispered Aileen.

"What?"

"That noise, a sort of sucking noise, do you not hear it?"

"You're imagining things."

But Aileen was not imagining anything. The noise grew louder until they were surrounded by squelchings and suckings as if a hundred giant boots were walking in wet mud. The mist began to lift and the children were relieved – but not for long. As the wisps cleared they saw that they were beside a swamp and the oily black muck was hiving with huge, white, slug-like creatures.

Some had already climbed out of the ooze and now stood on the edge balancing on short, stumpy legs. The legs supported fat bodies that rippled in rings of dough-white flesh and dripped with sticky goo. They were about six feet tall when standing upright and had no necks so that their ugly heads emerged straight from their thick bodies. They appeared to have no eyes at all, just a long tube-like snout with which they sniffed the air around them. In place of arms they had short seal-like flippers. Behind the advanced guard, smaller creatures were slurping to the surface of the swamp and crawling onto dry land. These had neither legs nor flippers and slid along like caterpillars, arching their backs in rippling loops.

The largest of the slugs, who seemed to be the leader, was waving its snout in the air as if it had caught the scent of something exciting. It nudged the other slugs until all the snouts were waving frantically and making sucking noises in the direction of the children.

They were trapped! Behind them was the precipice and on all sides were the slugs with their greedy snouts straining to suck them into the swamp. The fat white bodies began to move towards them, some walking upright on their stumps, others slithering around rocks and squeezing through crevices like toothpaste oozing from a tube.

The children had nothing with which to defend themselves except the stones that littered the ground. They began to throw with all their might but they knew it was useless. The stones bounced harmlessly off the spongy fat bodies. On and on they came, sucking at the ground and the air as they advanced. This is the end, thought Aileen. I think I would rather be in the lake with the eel.

With a sudden "whoosh" a hail of tiny arrows passed over the children's heads and plunged into the bulbous bodies of the leading slugs.

"Come over here!"

Aileen and Robin looked round but they could not see where the voice was coming from.

"Here, behind this rock."

A head was peeping out from behind a boulder and a dark-skinned finger was beckoning. They did not hesitate but rushed over to meet their rescuer. Behind the boulder were two weird little creatures no more than three feet high. More little heads peeped from behind every rock on the forlorn hillside.

"Are you dwarfs?" asked Aileen

"We are the Firslav, the Mountain People," answered an annoyed little person. "I am Duithnor the Life-Giver and this is my son, Lacklin. You have raised the Slobbolg and their maggot offspring. The swamp dwellers will crawl back to their pit now to lick their wounds but they will return. We must protect ourselves. Stay here and do not move until I tell you."

Duithnor began shouting orders to the other Firslav who scampered busily, obeying the barked directions. Since first stepping into the Otherworld, Aileen and Robin had come to realise that it was inhabited by many different species of people and creatures. The Firslav were short but very strong and agile. They wore sleeveless tunics that looked as if they had been woven from strands of raw wool left on briars by sheep as they wandered the mountain.

Pointed ears stood up from the sides of hairy faces and on Duithnor that hair was grey and thinning. The older Firslav had a little roly-poly belly but Lacklin, the son, had glossy black hair and his belly was flat and tight. All the Firslav wore hairy goatskin trousers – at least that is what the children thought at first. Then as the Firslav scampered over the rocks Aileen and Robin saw their black hooves. Were the Firslav people or mountain goats?

"Make yourselves useful," said Lacklin. "Gather as many stones as you can. Then watch my mother and wait for her word."

His cheek bones stood out high and proud from his

hairy face and they shone with the ruddy glow of fresh mountain air.

"We haven't done much damage," said Duithnor, "but we have gained a little time." Duithnor had a wise face. It was hairy but lacked the long beard that reached to her son's waist.

"The Slobbolg are blind and dull," she said. "They have great strength but they cannot think. They live in their quagmires until they are goaded into battle – then they fight to the death. The Firslav are not as strong as the Slobbolg, so we do not antagonise them. We live together in peace – usually. Now the Slobbolg have been roused and I know not why. We may not be strong enough for them."

While Duithnor was speaking her amber eyes scoured the souls of the children then they darted to her troops to supervise the battle plan. The Firslav were busy counting arrows and packing them neatly into skin pouches that they looped to their backs like school bags. The arrow heads were of sharp stone and were tied to the wooden shafts with thongs of leather. A finely tooled bow was hooked over every shoulder and a long curling horn dangled from every neck. An axe with a stone head was tucked into each belt.

"We are not warriors," said Lacklin. "We have not seen battle since the conquering of Balor. But we are good hunters and we have courage." He had the amber-gold eyes of his mother and he wore a tight-fitting leather helmet that tied somewhere beneath his beard. Although all the Firslav were hairy, some had long straggly beards and others had none so the children guessed that men and women were fighting side by side.

All the noise from the swamp had died down so Aileen peeked from behind the boulder to see what was happening. The surface of the swamp was calm and there was not a Slobbolg in sight. On the ground lay a large transparent object for all the world like a huge, empty plastic bag.

"What is that?" asked Aileen.

"We have killed one," answered Lacklin. "The wounded they take with them to heal in the swamp. The dead they drain with their snouts."

"Ugh!" shivered Robin.

"Gather up as much scree as you can," said Duithnor handing the children catapults made of leather and forked sticks. "A barrage of stones will distract them and allow us to take careful aim with our arrows."

Swiftly the children gathered a pile of sharp stones.

"Are you any good with a catapult?" asked Aileen.

"I dunno. I've never tried," answered Robin, "but I hope I'm a fast learner. I don't fancy being sucked inside out by those walking Hoovers."

✎ Escape! ✎

The words were hardly out of Robin's mouth when the terrifying slurp of large bodies emerging from the oily swamp brought a nervous silence to the Firslav camp.

"Hold fast!" instructed Lacklin. "Wait until they are within range then let loose with the catapults – as fast as you can."

The battle began and Aileen and Robin sent their stones flying through the air. They had no idea if they ever hit a Slobbolg but they certainly got better at using the catapults. The Firslav were leaping from rock to rock sending showers of arrows from every direction. Some of the giant slugs ignored the arrows embedded in their bodies, others pulled them out with their snouts and any who fell mortally wounded were surrounded by their fellow creatures and sucked dry until nothing remained but the loose outer skin.

The mountainside was alive with Firslav and the sky was dark with their tiny arrows but they had little effect on the Slobbolg. Some were wounded, one or two died but still they kept coming out of the swamp. It soon became clear that the Firslav could not stop the advance of the Slobbolg. Relentlessly they walked or crawled towards the boulder that sheltered the children.

"There is something about you mortals that is

driving them crazy," said Duithnor. "You must tell me what it is.

"Well, maybe she knows," said Robin uncertainly.

"Who knows what?"

"Maybe the Morrigan knows that we are trying to solve the Riddle." Quickly she told Duithnor about the Brod of Bres and the Riddle that would open the Evil Eye of Balor.

"Without doubt she knows and she has sent her creatures of the Underworld to stop you! We too have much to fear from the Morrigan. We must do all we can to thwart her evil plans. If the Eye is opened then the Firslav will be no more and base creatures will rule the worlds."

Duithnor thought for a moment then she spoke to Lacklin in a low voice and the Firslav's dark face seemed to pale.

"Follow Lacklin," said his mother turning to the children. "You must do exactly as he says and you must have courage. We Firslav can climb any cliff face and so we will escape from the Slobbolg but you are trapped. Go with my son, he will lead you to safety through the Weems."

Things moved so quickly now that children did not know what was happening. Lacklin told them to keep behind him, running as fast as they could, keeping their heads down and ignoring the Slobbolg no matter what they did. Then he began to dart and weave over the rock-strewn ground towards a shelf of bare rock. With their hearts pounding the children followed. They had to leave the shelter of the boulder and the protection of the Firslav and run over open ground across the path of the Slobbolg.

Being blind, the swamp creatures were at first unaware of what was happening but soon their snouts were sniffing out the human smell of the children and they came lumbering in pursuit. They were surprisingly fast for such huge, awkward creatures.

"Don't stop!" shouted Lacklin over his shoulder but the children could not keep up with the speed of his nimble goat feet. They ran as fast as their human feet would carry them.

From their rocky perches the Firslav were still shooting arrows but the Slobbolg had now moved out of the range of fire. Lacklin had reached the rock shelf and was urging the children on. Robin's throat was raw and sore with panting for breath but he thought he could make the shelf. Then he doubled up with a sharp pain in his side. It was a stitch but it felt like a stab from a sharp dagger.

"I can't go on!" he called to Aileen. She stopped and came back to help him.

"No, leave me," he said. "Get out of here."

Aileen looped his arm around her neck, grabbed his waist and began to drag him forward. Sensing victory the Slobbolg became very excited and their frenzied sucking noises closed in on the children. A white snout, as big as an elephant's trunk, slid round their waists and held them fast. They were lifted up in the air and squeezed until the breath was pushed out of them and they could see stars.

Through their dizziness the children saw Lacklin raise his arm and swing his axe. It hurtled through the air and struck the sensitive snout a severe blow. The Slobbolg dropped the children with such speed that they almost bounced off the ground. Then the Slobbolg nursed the injured snout under a flipper. The others ignored their injured brother and began to advance on Robin and Aileen.

Lacklin bounded down to them and pushed them to their feet.

"You must try or you will perish!"

The children did not think they had a drop of energy left but they stumbled on with Lacklin prodding and shouting at them. They could feel the snouts again sniffing and sucking and the hairs on their heads were lifted with the power of the suction. Up to the shelf they crawled but they were still within range of the snuffling snouts.

"In here," instructed Lacklin and he disappeared into the rock. The children inched forward on their hands and knees and they discovered a crack in the rock just wide enough to allow them to crawl through. They found themselves in a pitch-black cave. They collapsed on the rock floor and couldn't speak until their scorching lungs had time to settle.

"Are we safe here?" gasped Robin. He had seen the Slobbolg squeeze their blubbery bodies through smaller spaces and already their snouts were exploring the entrance to the dark cavern.

"We are safe from the Slobbolg now," answered Lacklin. "They need to stay near bog water or their skins will crack and split open. Besides they will not come into the Weems."

"What are the Weems?" asked Aileen.

"The Weems are the dark places; the home of the Lucorban and the slitherers."

Robin and Aileen couldn't believe their ears. They had met the Lucorban before and they never wanted to meet them again. They didn't like the sound of the slitherers either. Lacklin's eyes darted round the cavern and the children could see that he feared the Weems even more than the Slobbolg.

"Why did you come here?" asked Robin. "You could have escaped over the mountain with your people."

"But you couldn't," answered Lacklin. "You are standing in the way of the Morrigan and that makes you our kin. That clever piece of dragon-spit would make Weem slaves of the Firslav if she had the power so we must protect you if you are to succeed in your quest to challenge her Low Magic."

"So you brought us here to this cave even though it terrifies you?" queried Aileen.

"I have rescued you from the Slobbolg but you will not be safe until you have reached the Nameless Place. The journey is long and, as the Morrigan will have alerted her slaves to our presence in the Weems, it will be hazardous. For you, it was the only escape route from the swamp dwellers but now we may have worse problems to overcome."

"What do we do now?" asked Robin.

"We go forward to the Nameless Place, Mortal kids, and we will pray that the gods are watching over us."

Aileen looked at Robin and she saw that they shared the same silly thought. Lacklin was calling them "kids" but he meant young goats!

"If we are going on a long dangerous journey," she said, "then I think you should know our names. I'm Aileen and he's Robin."

Lacklin was sitting against the wall of the cave and he had left a "stranger" distance between himself and the children. Aileen got up and went over to him.

"We are very pleased to meet you," she said stretching out her hand. "And we are very grateful for what you have done for us."

Lacklin looked at her and his liquid gold eyes gleamed in the darkness. Then he smiled and the amusement crept up over his high cheek bones and crinkled round the slanted eyes.

"I am very pleased to meet you too, Aileen and Robin," he said and Aileen's hand was wrapped in a firm, warm grip. She knew instinctively that this was a friend she could trust with her life.

As it turned out, she had to do exactly that. A trip to the Weems should definitely not be included in a pleasant Saturday cross-country hike.

∞ The Weems ∞

The roof of the cavern was high where the children now stood but as it went further in it lowered and the walls closed in. It also grew very dark. This did not matter to Lacklin who could see perfectly in the dark but Robin and Aileen were stumbling all over the place until Robin remembered he had a torch in his rucksack. He hoped the batteries would outlast the journey!

Aileen did not like the dark passage they were now in. It smelled of blue-mould and it was getting narrower and narrower so that soon they had to hunch down and finally pull themselves along on their elbows. Robin was up ahead of her with the torch but they were packed so tightly into the tunnel that the light was no comfort at all. She could see little more than the soles of Robin's runners. The passage had to widen some time and when it did she was going to get in between Robin and Lacklin. Being last was not very pleasant – anything could come up behind her!

The rock was black and smooth as if it had been hollowed out by the saw-edged teeth of a giant rock-boring worm. It was cold and damp in the tunnel and there was little air. Drops of cold sweat dotted Aileen's brow and just when she felt she was going to suffocate she heard Lacklin's voice up ahead.

"We can rest here. You will find a little more room now."

The tunnel had widened out into a small grotto and there was indeed room for the children to sit upright.

"That tunnel wasn't made for the likes of us," said Robin looking ruefully at the torn sleeves of his tracksuit.

"All the entrances to the Weems are narrow," explained Lacklin. "Most would be too narrow for Mortal or Firslav."

"But the creatures who live in the Weems are not small are they?" asked Aileen remembering the Lucorban she met once before and who resembled giant cockroaches.

Lacklin smiled. "The Weem dwellers are shape-shifters. They can be as small as they like or as big. They are also clever. That is why the Firslav fear them more than they fear the Slobbolg."

"Have you ever been in the Weems before?" asked Robin.

"Yes," Lacklin replied and his voice grew sad. "My mother brought me here once with my brother Garwort when we were almost full-grown. The leader of the Firslav must be strong and wise and must know the secret haunts of the enemy. Avoiding warfare is the first duty of a leader and the second is to be prepared at all times to rebuff an enemy attack."

"Have you had many wars?" queried Aileen.

"Since Balor's Eye was closed by the young god Lugh all the peoples of the Otherworld have lived together peacefully. The creatures of the Underworld seek always to destroy this peace. The Morrigan is a warmonger and she commands their allegiance. The

Slobbolg would never have attacked you without her bidding. If she steals Balor's powers then all the peoples of the Otherworld will be her slaves and our lives will be torn apart by war and destruction. We must unite to stop her."

"You know your way through the Weems then?" said Robin bringing Lacklin back to the here and now. "I mean, you got through the last time you were here; the Weem creatures didn't get you."

"Yes, I escaped the fury of the slitherers and the Lucorban – but my brother Garwort did not. The Weem people do not like trespassers and they show them no mercy."

As he spoke a tear gathered in the corner of Lacklin's tawny eye and rolled down into his beard. Aileen reached out and stroked the long black hairs on the back of his hand. She couldn't find a word to say but Lacklin seemed comforted by her touch.

"If we are to get through the Weems safely and reach the Nameless Place then we must be swift," he said, and he was off before the children could ask where this Nameless Place was.

The passage was broader now and they could walk upright. They were walking uphill at quite a steep angle and the floor was wet and slippery. Aileen was sandwiched between Robin and Lacklin and she felt safer than she had in the tunnel. Gradually the passage broadened and then opened into a wide chamber. A layer of pure white rock ran diagonally across the black walls so that the children felt they were walking through a liquorice allsort. The chamber branched into three identical tunnels.

"Which way do we go now?" asked Robin.

Lacklin moved towards one passage and began feeling the wall with his long fingers. Then he shook his head and tried another passage.

"What's the matter?" asked Aileen. "I thought you knew the way?"

"Many years have passed since first I wove my way through the Weems. There has been much new burrowing. We marked our path in the softer white rock but I cannot find the mark. It may have been obliterated."

"What kind of mark is it?" asked Aileen.

"It's a simple triangle and a circle. The mark of the Firslav – the sun rising over the mountain top."

They took a passage each and began to feel slowly and carefully over the surface of the white rock.

"Bring the torch over here," called Aileen. "I think I have found something."

"There's some sort of a mark there all right," said Robin, "but it's very faint. How long is it since you made the mark, Lacklin?"

"In Mortal time?" asked Lacklin. "Well, I suppose about a thousand years give or take a century or two."

"It's not much like a sun rising over a mountain but it's all there is," said Robin. "I vote we go this way."

And so they continued along the middle passage. They were still climbing but it was a comfortable walk as the passage was wide enough to allow them to walk three abreast.

Lacklin looked worried.

"There are many paths through the Weems," he said, "but it is easy to get lost and there are places to be avoided."

The beam from Robin's torch lit their way and cast

weird shadows. Beyond the light, deep darkness closed in and held unknown dangers.

A deathly rattle echoed through the passage. The trio halted and listened. The echo came again.

"What is it?" whispered Robin.

"The Lucorban," answered Lacklin. "They know we are here."

"Are they in front or behind?" queried Aileen remembering with horror the vicious crab-clawed creatures that had attacked her near Killyshee Wood.

"Wherever they are, we must go forward," decided Lacklin. "It is our only chance of escape."

Out of the darkness came a sinister scuffling and scuttling and ahead of them a forest of claws waved menacingly in the beam of the torch.

"They are behind us too!" gasped Robin. "We are trapped!"

"Shine your light on those behind us," ordered Lacklin. "Their eyes are used to darkness and they will be blinded for a while."

Robin swung the torch at the Lucorban. The beam lit up their ugly leathery faces and the deadly fangs jutting over thick lips. The tiny eyes, almost lost in pouches of loose skin, blinked against the pain of the light and the armour-plated bodies rattled as they clashed into each other in a confusion of snapping pincers.

Lacklin took the horn that hung from his neck and raised it to his lips. A low hum came from the horn and then it grew louder and louder and skirled through the children's ear drums until they were in danger of exploding. Still Lacklin blew, his cheeks puffed and straining. The noise rose to a higher pitch and the children clutched at their ears in pain. Then suddenly they could no longer hear it. Lacklin was still blowing and now the Lucorban were convulsing in pain.

"Why can't we hear it, Robin?" whispered Aileen.

"I think maybe the sound has gone out of the range of human hearing," replied Robin also in a whisper. "But the Lucorban can hear it all right. It's driving them mad!"

The over-grown cockroaches were scuttling away in retreat from the agonising sound.

Perspiration was dripping from Lacklin's leather helmet and he collapsed on the floor of the passage, his chest heaving in great gasps.

"That will hold them for a while," he said when he had recovered sufficiently to speak, "but I will not be able to blow the horn at the Third Level again."

"The Third Level?" queried Aileen.

"The horn has three ranges," explained Lacklin. "The First the Firslav use to communicate with each other, the Second with the other peoples of the Otherworld, and the Third we use to inflict punishment on our Fomar enemies if they attack us. It takes great strength to blow at the Third Level. When all the Firslav blow together it is easier but for one alone it is a tremendous feat and cannot be repeated."

"Are they still out there?" asked Robin.

"The horn blow is still echoing through the tunnels although you Mortals cannot hear it. The Lucorban will have scattered to larger chambers where the blast is not so powerful. Soon it will have died away and they will be after us again. Our only chance is to find another tunnel that will take us past them before they have time to re-group. Swiftness of foot is needed now."

They ran, shining the torch wildly over ceiling and walls, but it was the sharp eye of Lacklin that spotted the small opening high up in the wall.

"It looks very narrow," he said. "It could be a wormhole that is not yet completed and may lead nowhere but we must take the chance."

Lacklin stood back from the wall and bunched his wiry body like a coiled spring. Then he gave a powerful leap and grabbed the lip of the opening with his strong fingers. His hooved feet skittered quickly up the smooth wall and he was safely in the hole. The children could not leap into the air, nor had they hooved feet and they stared upwards in dismay. Two disembodied eyes gleamed in the darkness above their heads.

"Aileen, you stand on my hands and I will give you a heave up," ordered Robin.

"But what about you?"

"We'll get you up first and worry about me later."

Robin switched off the torch and tucked it in his pocket for safety. Then he cupped his hands to receive Aileen's feet. Robin heaved, Aileen strained and Lacklin stretched out his arms. Aileen felt herself soaring through the darkness. Her arms flailed helplessly in the empty air and then Lacklin's strong hands wrapped themselves round her wrists.

Getting Robin up was even more of an acrobatic feat. This time Lacklin held Aileen by the ankles and suspended her over the edge so that her fingers hovered over Robin's but still she could not reach him.

"Take off your rucksack," gasped Aileen, "and stand on it."

Robin was reluctant to abandon his rucksack but an ominous rattle from behind changed his mind. He put

71

his compass in his other pocket and threw the rucksack on the ground. It gave him the extra inches that he needed. He grasped Aileen's hands and spider-walked up the wall as Lacklin hauled them both into the hole.

The wormhole grew so narrow that it would have been impossible for Robin to wear the rucksack anyway so he didn't feel so bad about leaving it. The children had to turn over on their backs and wriggle forward by pushing with heels and bottoms and levering with the palms of their hands on the roof. To protect their skinned noses they turned their faces to the wall and prayed that they would have enough air to keep them alive. The torch was wedged in Robin's pocket and the utter darkness was the worst part of their struggle towards the unknown.

If this hole leads nowhere, thought Aileen, I'm going to stay here and become a fossil. I'm not squirming back to meet the Lucorban!

A surprised grunt from Lacklin should have alerted her but Aileen was not prepared for the sudden ending of the tunnel and so she screamed aloud as she tumbled down a slope of sharp chippings onto Lacklin's sprawled furry body. With a painful thump Robin came crashing down on top of her, squashing her into a sandwich filling. They sorted themselves out and gingerly Robin removed the torch from his pocket and switched it on. The broad beam illuminated a startling scene.

They were in a chamber as vast as a football stadium. Hexagonal pillars of black basalt towered to a vaulted roof that dripped long, pale, petrified icicles. A broad swathe of white rock coiled round the black pillars and twisted and soared upwards in a pattern of whirls. There were whirls within whirls and tall spikes that were the needle-sharp remnants of ancient spirals. Below their feet the spirals continued down into an endless blackness. They stood on a narrow ledge connected to the crazy natural sculpture by a fragile bridge of white rock. As they stared in wonder the white rock began to glow with a blue light and waves of sound whooshed through cavities and spirals. The children felt like tiny insects imprisoned inside a giant sea-worn whelk shell.

"The Wentel Trap," said Lacklin and the children knew by his sombre voice and solemn face that he was not announcing good news.

"What's this now?" asked Robin. "Are we out of the frying pan and into the fire again?"

∽ The Wentel Trap ∽

"Lacklin," said Aileen to the woebegone Firslav, "just exactly what is the Wentel Trap?"

"I had hoped to bring you to the Nameless Place without entering the Wentel Trap," sighed Lacklin, "but I have failed."

The little goatman looked so miserable and downcast that Aileen had to put her arm round his drooping shoulders.

"There you go again," she said. "Wentel Trap, Nameless Place – we don't know what you're talking about."

"The Nameless Place is at the top of the Mountain," said a despondent Lacklin. "We will find an exit from the Weems there and you will be safe."

"And The Wentel Trap?"

"The Wentel Trap is the den of the slitherers – the Vilesvart. It is a most terrible place. There is a way out but it is almost impossible to find it before the Vilesvart find you. It was here my brother perished. We had warned him to stay by us but Garwort was young and headstrong. He wandered off by himself. We heard his screams – I hear them still – and we knew he was caught in the Wentel Trap. I fear we may never see daylight again."

"We won't if we don't try," said Robin. "You say that the Nameless Place is at the top of the mountain so the exit must be up there somewhere. We've got to start climbing!"

As he spoke, Robin looked up. It was a terrifying height but there were plenty of footholds in the sculptured rock. One slip however and they would plunge headlong into the abyss to be impaled on a forest of spikes. The rocks shimmered and throbbed and filled the Wentel Trap with their cold, blue light.

"At least we can see where we're going," said Robin switching off his torch. "Come on, there's no point in standing around."

Aileen looked at Robin gratefully. Lacklin's depression had alarmed her and for the first time she really felt that she would never be home again. Now Robin had cheered her and she wanted to do the same for Lacklin.

"Robin's right, Lacklin," she said. "We have to try. Nothing's impossible. We'll get out all right."

The Firslav smiled. "You are courageous for Mortals," he said. "I have not lost heart. I was filled with a great sadness for my brother. We will go up."

Carefully they crossed the narrow bridge and began to climb. The white rock burned like solid ice and the children's feet and fingers ached with the numbing cold. The lacy pattern of whirls and spindles was dangerous but convenient for climbing. Up they went into the spiral, resting in the curved hollows and using the worn cavities as footholds. Aileen tried not to look down. She knew that one glimpse of the yawning chasm bristling with spikes and she would lose her footing.

They made good progress and the children began to hope that they would find the exit before the Vilesvart found them. Robin grasped a spindle of rock to pull himself up and then he screamed. The spindle had changed shape and in his hand writhed a yellow and black striped snake!

"Drop it!" shouted Lacklin. "It has poison enough to kill a great elk stag."

Robin didn't need to be told twice. The horned viper bared its hooked fangs as Robin flung it far out into the purple darkness of the abyss. That was only the start. The Wentel Trap began to throb with hissings and rattlings.

"They are everywhere!" said Aileen.

And they were. Snakes of every size and colour dangled from cavities, coiled in hollows or corkscrewed up spikes. Some were tiny and gathered in writhing heaps of twisted bodies; others were as long as a bus or as thick as a tree trunk. They looped their sinuous bodies through holes and round stumps of rock as if they were playing a game. None of the reptiles seemed inclined to attack the three intruders. They were content to coil and hiss and watch with their glittering eyes.

"Why don't they come and get us and get it all over with!" shouted Aileen almost in hysterics.

"They are enjoying our fear," answered Lacklin. "They want to see what we will do."

"There's nothing we can do, is there?" asked Robin. "No matter which way we turn they're there."

The three were cowering in the curve of a spiral just big enough to hold them. As far up or down as they could see, the Wentel Trap was infested with the slithering Vilesvart.

"What about your horn?" suggested Robin.

"Useless," replied Lacklin. "Even if I had the strength it wouldn't work in a large chamber like this."

They sat with their feet tucked underneath their bottoms and the Vilesvart slithered lazily round their tiny refuge. Now and again one would wrap its tail round a spike and dangle over their heads to taunt them with flickering tongue and bared fangs. If one of them screamed in fear then the Vilesvart wriggled away with what seemed to be a contented grin on its face. This continued for some time but then the hissing and rattling grew louder and more persistent and the Vilesvart began to mass closer.

"They grow tired of their game," said Lacklin, rising to his feet. "We can either sit here and wait for them to swarm over us or go into the attack. I am a Firslav and I will die like one!"

At that moment an ugly head, patterned with red and black zigzags, dangled above them. The brave little goatman had no weapons left with which to fight but he wrapped his arm round the neck of the Vilesvart and squeezed with all his might. The reptile squirmed fiercely and lost its tail hold. Lacklin dashed it against a rock and then sent it flying out into the dark.

Rage hissed through the Wentel Trap and many hundreds of angry heads waved in the air and stretched towards the little Firslav. He stood and faced them bravely, prepared to kill more before their poison stopped him. Aileen and Robin now stood with their backs against the white rock. The situation was hopeless.

∞ The Nameless Place ∞

"Help! Help!"

Aileen's frantic cries echoed through the grottoes of the Wentel Trap.

"That'll do a lot of good," grunted Robin.

Lacklin was struggling with the muscular contortions of a shiny black Vilesvart and he was losing. The reptile was wrapped round the Firslav and it was only a matter of moments before the breath of life was crushed out of him. The Vilesvart had swarmed in a squirming tangle of flailing tails, darting tongues and violent colours. They carpeted every surface of the Wentel Trap so that the blue light of the rocks was blotted out and Robin again had to use the torch.

It was useless crying for help; Aileen knew that. There was no one to hear her but she had to do something. She was about to cry out again when the faintest sound came floating into her head. It was a voice – the very small voice of Cathara and she could see the sincere face of her tiny Annalaire friend as she said, "Whenever you need our help, you only have to wish for it."

Were the Annalaire telepathic or was she just remembering a promise made? Aileen didn't know but she had nothing to lose so she closed her eyes tightly and she pictured Cathara and Allochar and from the very depths of her being she begged for their help.

Nothing happened. Lacklin was almost breathing his last and a phalanx of raised heads, poised for the kill, encircled Robin and Aileen. Then the most beautiful music came soughing through the Weems. Unearthly notes plucked by spirit hands from ghostly harps and soothing drifts of elfin piping wafted through the chambers and cavities of the Wentel Trap. The haunting music was at once joyous and unbearably sad.

"The music of the Shee!" wheezed Lacklin as the Vilesvart loosed its grip and slithered away. "I have heard it only once in my life and I have never forgotten it. It is magic music that can lure away a loved one or lull an enemy to slumber. Look!" he said pointing to the Vilesvart.

All around them the entranced Vilesvart swayed to the hypnotic effects of the music!

"They are mesmerised, like snakes by a snake charmer!" exclaimed Robin.

Some hooded eyes drooped and closed, others were open but glazed; some flat heads disappeared under tails, others remained upright see-sawing gently but without threat. This, Aileen was sure, was the answer to her fervent plea and silently she sent a heartfelt "thank you" to the Annalaire.

"The Shee music will not last long," declared Lacklin. "We must take our chance to escape."

"But everywhere is thick with Vilesvart!" exclaimed Aileen. "How are we going to get past them?"

"They will not harm us as long as the music is playing. We must climb over them."

This was the most horrifyingly disgusting thing the

children had ever had to do. Just imagine crawling over a web of intertwining serpents! Gingerly Aileen put her foot out and tried to stand on the firm back of one of the largest reptiles but her foot slipped and she sank. She was up to her waist in writhing bodies!

Robin had already begun his climb towards the roof.

"Give me your hand," he said and he reached down and hoisted her up beside him.

Up they journeyed towards the roof of the Wentel Trap, using the Vilesvart as living stepladders. It was a journey that is the stuff of nightmares. Although dazed, the slitherers were not unconscious and they rolled and twisted to the children's touch. Surprisingly the skins were not cold and slimy as the children expected but were warm and dry under their fingers. Venomous heads swayed at them and glazed eyes stared unwinking, only inches from their faces.

"We must not hesitate!" warned Lacklin.

Aileen would have liked to close her eyes but she was scared of slipping and tumbling down to be buried in the heaving mass of Vilesvart. Heads swung at her from nowhere, startling her and causing her to cry out. Tongues flicked lazily over her face. The strange music still sighed dreamily around them and Aileen prayed that it would continue until they were free from this poisonous pit.

"Look!" shouted Robin. "Up ahead! Look!"

Aileen raised her head and she could see it. Far up in the darkness, like a lonely star, shone a pinpoint of light. It was natural light too, not the eerie blue that had come from the rocks. But it was very far away and the children had to endure their spiralling climb over the Vilesvart bodies for a long time before they could crawl into the lighted tunnel that they hoped would take them to freedom.

Lacklin was last into the tunnel and his hooves had no sooner clattered onto the bare rock than the Shee music stopped. Aileen was leading the trio this time and she did not need Lacklin's shouted order to propel herself forward towards the daylight. Their way was still not clear. This was the beginning of the spiral that formed the Wentel Trap and so it twisted tightly towards the surface.

"They are in the tunnel!" warned Lacklin.

Frantically they twisted and turned but the spiral got tighter as they approached its apex.

"We can't fail now!" screamed Aileen. "I can see the sky!"

But she was stuck fast.

"Move," gasped Robin, "or we're caught!"

"I can't," wailed Aileen and the tears were streaming down her face. A shadow blotted out the daylight and suddenly she was wrenched forward out of the tunnel and into the sweet fresh air.

Strong Firslav arms helped to steady her on her feet and Firslav voices chattered excitedly around her.

"Robin! Lacklin!" she cried but the strong arms had already pulled them both to safety.

"Will they come after us?" asked Robin as the tunnel filled with angry hissings and glittering eyes.

"No," replied Lacklin. "The Vilesvart dislike the sunlight and rarely emerge whilst it is still day."

The children found themselves almost at the very tip top of Cloughderg Mountain. They were standing on a broad platform of rock high above Lough Foyle. Behind them a great hump of bare black rock soared straight up and then ended abruptly in a flat top. Below them spread the great panorama of the wide-mouthed river and far to the west they could see the stark outline of Grianan Fort. Right on the edge of the platform stood the Stone of the Curses. Other great slabs were scattered around the platform forming a giant table of stone. This then was the burial place of the son of the Dagda; the place the Firslav called "Nameless".

Aileen's first instinct was to rush to the Stone of the Curses and examine it minutely but the Firslav were crowding round them patting their backs and dancing with glee. Then the crowd fell silent and moved aside. At the edge of the crowd stood Duithnor and her old face beamed her happiness. Lacklin walked forward and went down on one knee before his chief and mother.

"I am glad to see Duithnor safe from the Slobbolg," he said bowing his head.

Duithnor reached down and raised her son to his feet. Then she wrapped him in her sinewy arms.

"Welcome, Lacklin," she whispered through her tears. "We thought we had lost you to the Weem dwellers. You will make a strong and courageous leader of the Firslav when I am gone."

There was a lot of throwing back of heads and whooping in high coarse bleats, which the children supposed was a Firslav form of cheering, before they could break away to examine the Stone. It stood about eight feet in height and a circular hole, about the size of a man's fist, was bored right through the middle. Aileen stood on tiptoe and put her hand through it and waved it about.

"I wonder what this is for?" she puzzled.

"I dunno," answered Robin, "and there's nothing red

about it is there?"

"No," agreed Aileen contemplating the grey, speckled Stone.

At that moment the evening sun came out from behind a pile of black clouds and thousands of tiny crystals, that had formed in the Stone millions of years ago, glinted like precious jewels – but it still wasn't red.

Robin turned and stood with his back to the Stone and faced the hump of bare rock that formed the summit of Cloughderg Mountain.

"It must be in there," he said.

"What?" asked Aileen absentmindedly as she poked around the Stone.

"The Eye of course, Balor's Eye. It must be in there somewhere."

Quickly Aileen turned and stared. Robin was right. The hump of rock had to be the petrified head of Balor with its one awful Eye. Slowly she recited the Riddle of the Opening of the Evil Eye.

When Moon doth wax and Sun rides high
The time of reckoning is nigh.
As light doth pierce the Cursèd Stone,
When new life's bud by Death be borne,
If Two-in-One in place are twined
Keep vigil and watch as the Eye unwinds.

Here was the Eye and the Morrigan had the Brod of Bres – the Two-in-One. They had found the Eye but they were well behind the wicked Shape-shifter in the quest to solve the Riddle. Aileen shuddered and suddenly she felt the piercing cold of the mountain air.

"We must leave the Nameless Place, Aileen and

Robin," said Lacklin interrupting the girl's thoughts. "It is a place of unspeakable deeds and restless spirits; we do not like to tarry long here."

The Firslav led the children down the mountain by a safe path, a path that did not skirt Lough Shule nor disturb the Slobbolg. It was also a very quick route and less steep than the one they had climbed. In no time at all they were off the mountain and on familiar ground.

"Now it is time to say farewell," said Lacklin and he held out his strong, hard hand.

Aileen ignored the hand and flung her arms round the flustered Firslav's neck. "We owe you so much," she said, "and we might never see you again!"

Lacklin patted her back and murmured in a voice gruff with emotion, "Our two worlds are not meant to meet. What has brought us together I do not know. Much has happened today that I do not understand. We do not know what the future may hold. We may meet again, my friend with the yellow hair."

Robin came forward and shook hands with Lacklin and then the children bowed formally to Duithnor. With a whoop of glee the Firslav were off scampering up the mountain, back to their own airy world.

Robin and Aileen too had to return to their world and explain the lateness of the hour and the loss of a rucksack.

∽ Treachery! ∽

"Would you look at the state of you!" demanded Aileen's mother. Claire Scroggy looked pale and tired and Aileen felt a pang of guilt.

"Where were you till this hour?"

Aileen didn't answer. How could she? No one would believe a word she said and she was too exhausted to think up a reasonable story.

"We need to be thinking of your mother now and not be worrying her," said Tom Scroggy as he stretched his legs in front of the fire. Tom's voice was mild and there was no hint of anger in his eyes but Aileen was full of guilt and resentment and she just couldn't control her tongue.

"I don't need you to be telling me what to do," she said, bursting into tears. "You're not my father!"

There was a horrified silence in the room for a few seconds and then Claire found her voice.

"Go to your room, Aileen!" she ordered.

Aileen stood sobbing loudly but she didn't move. She had never seen her mother so upset before. Her lips were white and a dangerous flush was creeping into her pale face. She was struggling to lift her heavy body from the straight backed chair.

"This minute!" she shouted as she saw Aileen's hesitation.

"Settle yourself, love," said Tom rising in alarm to comfort his sobbing wife.

"I think you'd better do as your mother says, Aileen, and go to your room," said Aggie Scroggy softly as she poured some dark liquid into a glass for her mother. There was kindness and understanding in the old woman's face but Aileen was too miserable to see it. Reluctantly, she left the room. She always seemed to say or do the wrong thing. There were so many thoughts crowding through her head but she couldn't get them in order. She loved her mother and didn't mean to hurt her but there was something raw and sore deep inside her that made her angry.

Aileen stood in the hall with her back against the door and she heard the murmurs in the room. She heard Tom's deep, steady voice.

"Don't be getting yourself into a state, Claire. The wee girl didn't mean what she said. Sure she's only a bit of a wean," he coaxed.

"Maybe," sniffled her mother, "but I'm worried about her all the same. She's not like my Aileen any more. Look at her today – she never stayed out as late as that before in her life."

"It's not all that late," replied Tom. "Living in the country's different from town – it's easy to forget the time when you're out over the mountain. This time of the year's the worst when the sun never seems to set. I was always forgetting to come home and many's the hiding I got. Isn't that right, Ma?"

"Indeed he's right, Claire," agreed Aggie. "He had the heart scalded out of me."

"'Midsummer madness' my father used to call it."

Claire laughed softly at the idea of Tom being a

botheration to his parents.

"Aileen will be all right when she gets herself sorted out," assured Aggie. "There's that much happening to her at the moment that she can't make head nor tail of it."

Up in her room Aileen sat on the window-sill feeling very sorry for herself. She was an outsider in the house; a Kennedy in the middle of a hive of Scroggys. Her mother was all taken up with the baby and so were Tom and his mother. They would be far happier if she wasn't there at all. Her mother couldn't really love her or she wouldn't have looked for another family – another baby. She reached over to her dressing table and lifted her father's picture. It was the only one of him she had. She didn't remember her dad at all but she missed him. She looked at the smiling boyish face, the studded leather jacket and the motorbike gleaming with care and love. Only a few weeks after the photo was taken the bike was a wreck and Paul Kennedy gone. She nursed the photograph to her heart and she felt very close to her dad – two Kennedys together.

It was still daylight outside although it was after half past ten. A big moon shone in the pale violet sky so that it was possible to see everything clearly. It was very calm and the few cotton-wool clouds were streaked pink by the rays of the sun as it dipped below the hills at the far side of the Lough. The Foyle was a pond of molten gold.

Something niggled at the back of Aileen's mind. It was something Tom Scroggy said; something about the sun never setting and Midsummer madness.

Of course! Midsummer! The longest day of the year when the sun was at its highest point above the equator giving summer to the northern hemisphere. She had learned all about it in school. The first lines of the Riddle sprang into her head.

When Moon doth wax and Sun rides high
The time of reckoning is nigh.

That was it! The sun would be at its highest point in the sky on the twenty-first of June! But what about the moon? Aileen looked at the pale orb as it sailed across the night sky. It was big but it was not full. She leapt from the sill and began to search feverishly for the diary that she always meant to fill but never did. It took her a few minutes to find it and a few seconds to turn to the twentieth of June. There on the top left-hand corner of the page was a full moon. There would be a full moon on the eve of Midsummer! While the moon waxed full the sun would rise to its highest point in the northern sky! It was only two days until Midsummer Eve.

Another piece of the puzzle had fallen into place. She now knew where and when the Eye of Balor could be opened. She also knew part of the how. The Brod of Bres had to be placed somewhere, that much was clear, but what did the other part mean?

When new life's bud by Death is borne

Aileen tortured her brain with thinking but she could come up with no sensible answer. She hoped that the Morrigan was stuck at that part of the Riddle too. I'm too tired now to think straight, she decided. I'll talk it over with Robin tomorrow. Sleepiness then came on her so fast that she just tumbled under her duvet, dirty tracksuit and all, and fell into a deep slumber. She was still clutching the photograph of her father.

Aileen sat up with a jerk. The room was dark and cold. Something had wakened her but all was still and silent. Then she heard a slight noise. She held her breath and waited. There it was again – a light "ting" on glass. Someone was throwing pebbles at her window. She pushed the duvet aside and crept to the window-sill. There was someone out there standing under the damson tree. The shadowed figure was tall and she couldn't see a face. She was just about to call her mother when the figure stepped out from under the tree.

At that moment the moon came out from behind a cloud and lit the upraised face. It was the face from the photograph! The man under the damson tree was her father! The youthful face smiled a divil-may-care grin and the shoulder-length fair hair curled around the collar of the leather jacket.

"Come with me, Aileen," spoke her father and, although she could not remember his voice, she knew that that was exactly how it would have sounded.

"Come on, Aileen," he coaxed. "We'll go for a spin and I'll have you back before they wake up. You won't even be missed."

These last words were all that Aileen needed. She wouldn't be missed, she told herself, if she never came back at all. She pushed the window up and slid over the sill and down into the arms of her father. A rush of happiness choked her, leaving her unable to speak.

"Look," said her father pointing towards the tree and

there, in all its glittering glory, stood the motorbike from the photograph.

Aileen climbed onto the bike and wrapped her arms around the studded jacket and then, with the roar of a lion, they were off. It didn't occur to Aileen that the noise had failed to waken anyone in the house. Down the lane they streaked and then they began to go cross-country over hilly terrain. The ground was rough and rock-strewn but the powerful bike seemed to fly over all obstacles without as much as a bump. The wind tore through Aileen's hair and she wanted to sing out with joy. On and on they roared through the darkness until Aileen lost track of time and place. She never wanted that ride to end.

The motorbike finally ground to a halt and Aileen found herself lifted from the pillion and placed gently on the ground. She was in a strange place; a place she had never seen before. It was very dark except for the dull luminance of the moonshine trapped behind a layer of cloud. It took Aileen's eyes a while to adjust to the darkness and then she saw a bleak scene that belonged more to an undiscovered planet than to earth. They were standing on a flat plain with not a bush, nor tree, nor blade of grass in sight. Jagged, misshapen rocks punctured the dusty plain as if they had been blasted there by an explosion in space or thrown by a giant hand. It was an ugly place and Aileen began to feel uneasy. She also felt very cold.

"You are very unhappy, aren't you, Aileen?"

The voice was just as coaxing as it had been earlier. Aileen looked at her father but she could no longer see his face properly. A halo of blue light was dancing round his head, throwing his face into shadow.

"I can make things right for you, if you'll let me," said her father. "Wouldn't you like to have your mother to yourself again with no one to love but you?"

Aileen couldn't trust herself to speak so she nodded dumbly. The cold grew more intense. The blue light danced towards Aileen so that she too was wrapped in its halo. The cold penetrated her body and she felt herself begin to freeze inside.

"You will have to do something for me first," said her father. "Something that I'm sure you won't mind doing. Then everything will be as it was and you will be back living with your mother in Drumenny. Will you help me, Aileen?"

Her father's dark shape shimmered through the blue glow and, for a moment, Aileen thought she saw his shape quiver and change into something vaguely familiar. But the light steadied and she saw once again the cheeky, appealing grin.

"Please, Aileen," her father pleaded. "I really need your help. If you do as I ask then I can make all your dreams come true."

The heartfelt plea and her desire to have her life the way she wanted were great temptations for Aileen. But still she hesitated. Other voices were tugging at her; they came from far away in time and in place.

"With your help I can change anything, Aileen. We can all be together again – you, me and your mother."

This dream was beyond even Aileen's wildest hopes and the very idea of it was just too much for her. She hesitated no longer. Eagerly she nodded her head in agreement. At that moment a sliver of ice embedded itself in her heart.

The blue light now began to pulsate madly, flashing

wildly around the dark figure that had been her father. The light grew more intense and Aileen had to shade her eyes. In the white-cold dazzling centre of the light she saw her father's shape tremble and change. Then everything stilled and out of the light appeared a three-headed monster. One head was that of a vicious beaked bird, another that of a spitting serpent and the one in the middle was that of a beautiful woman. It was the Morrigan – the worricow, the Shape-shifter.

"You are mine now, Aileen the Fair," the beautiful face said solemnly. "We have made a bargain, you and I."

Again Aileen nodded obediently.

Aileen jumped and the photograph crashed out of her hand and onto the floor. She was frozen to the marrow but her brow was drenched in sweat. She'd had a nightmare; the worst nightmare she'd ever had. She got out of the bed and picked up the photograph. The glass was smashed to smithereens and she could not see her father's face through the clouded splinters.

She looked at her tattered tracksuit and remembered all that had happened to herself and Robin on Cloughderg Mountain. She went to her dressing table and looked in the mirror. There was something different about her face. Her blue eyes seemed cold and distant. She remembered too her great discovery about Midsummer's Eve. She was going to tell Robin about it in the morning. Maybe I'll keep it to myself, she thought as she got into her nightdress and climbed back into bed. It's none of his business anyway.

She was cold in bed but it was not a body cold that could be cured with blankets. It was an inside cold that numbed her soul.

∞ A New Arrival ∞

All through Sunday Aileen stayed in her room and her
mother felt that maybe she was better left alone for a
while. Robin Drake called for her in the afternoon but
he was told that Aileen wasn't feeling well and he went
away puzzled. He was sure that Aileen would have
been bursting to talk about their adventures of the day
before and their plans for solving the rest of the Riddle
and finishing their project.

On Monday Aileen got up at eight as usual, ate her
breakfast in silence and left for school. Robin was
already at the bus stop when she got there and he said
a cheery good morning. Aileen nodded in reply and
then began to search through her school bag for an
imaginary something or other so that she wouldn't
have to talk to him. Robin got the message – especially
when she sat by herself in the bus and went to an
empty table in the classroom. He was puzzled and hurt.
At lunchtime Aileen had her sandwiches with her arch-
enemies, Nuala Deery and Lisa McCarron, leaving
Robin on his lonely seat by the wall overlooking a
turnip field.

After school, when the bus drew up at the lane,
Aileen jumped out quickly and ran off before Robin
even put a foot to the ground. As she hurried up the

slope of the lane a hoot from a car startled her and almost sent her tumbling into the ditch. She recognised the local doctor as he waved cheerily at her and disappeared round a bend. Another strange car was parked in the yard and in the kitchen a fat woman in a nurse's uniform was tucking into a large slice of Aggie Scroggy's sponge cake. Aggie herself was pouring tea from the best china teapot and two bright red dots glowed in her waxy cheeks.

"Ah, Aileen," she said in a breathless fluster, "there you are. There's great news!"

It was the first time Aileen had ever seen Aggie Scroggy in a dither and she watched as the old woman poured tea until it overflowed into the saucer.

"What's happened? Is Mammy all right?" asked Aileen.

"Go on upstairs and see for yourself," grinned Aggie. "You have a lovely wee brother."

"But the baby's not supposed to come for another two or three weeks!"

"Babies have a habit of doing what they're not supposed to do."

Aileen pushed open the bedroom door and stood there not moving. Her mother was propped up in the brass-railed bed and she looked more relaxed than she had done in weeks. Tom Scroggy was standing beside the bed holding a white bundle as if it was going to take a bite out of him. A stupid grin was plastered all over his face.

"Come in, Aileen love," smiled her mother, "and meet your wee brother."

"Are you all right, Mammy?" asked Aileen going straight to the bed.

"I'm fine," laughed her mother. "I don't think I ever felt better. Wait till you see him! There's a look of you about him, so there is. Tom, let Aileen hold the baby."

"There you are – born on a Midsummer Eve – that will bring him good luck," laughed Tom and the bundle was thrust into Aileen's arms. She looked at the blotchy face, the tightly closed eyes and the perfect rosebud mouth.

"Very nice," she said and handed the baby straight back to a surprised Tom. Out of the corner of her eye Aileen could see her mother's face crumple in disappointment.

The rest of the day went by in a blur. There was the milking to be done and the evening meal to get ready and after that Hugh Bradley called in with Rosaleen and Robin. They had come to see the new baby. The kitchen was busy with tea-making and sandwich-cutting and bottles of frothing stout had to be opened to wet the baby's head. Robin sat at the end of the table nibbling a sandwich and sipping a glass of Coke. Aileen was polite to him, asking if he wanted more Coke and that, but then she ignored him.

When the tea had been handed out and the baby admired and examined for familiar features and the "oohs and the ahs" said about the weight of him, Aggie Scroggy took a minute to have a good look at Aileen. The girl was behaving very well but there was something disquieting about her expressionless face. She went over to Aileen on the pretext of asking her to pass more cake around. As she stooped towards the girl she looked into her eyes. She saw a coldness there that troubled her deeply.

"I wonder if you would come with me, Robin," said

Aggie turning to the boy, "and give me a hand to shut up the hens."

Robin was glad to escape from the kitchen. The hens were already roosting on their perches in the henhouse and Robin knew that Aggie didn't really need his help. However, he propped the plank up against the door to keep out the foxes and placed stones at the base of it to steady it.

"Robin," said Aggie when they had finished their work, "has something happened? I mean, have you and Aileen been doing battle with the Morrigan again?"

Robin wasn't surprised at Aggie's question. The old woman always seemed to know everything that was going on. She had helped himself and Aileen when they had been in danger from the Morrigan before and so he told her the whole story of the Riddle of Balor's Eye and their journey through the Weems.

"I heard the story of Balor when I was a child," mused Aggie, "but I've never come across the Riddle before. And you think the Morrigan has the Brod of Bres?"

Robin nodded.

"I think you're probably right. And with that in her possession she will stop at nothing to open the Eye."

Again Robin agreed and Aggie had another question for him.

"Does Aileen seem different in any way today?"

This time Robin was surprised.

"Yes, there *is* something very odd about her but I can't put my finger on it."

"I have looked into her eyes and I have seen the mark of the Morrigan. I fear Aileen has come under her power. She is now the Morrigan's slave and will do whatever is asked of her."

"That's not possible!" protested Robin. "We met the Morrigan's horrible creatures on Cloughderg Mountain but we didn't see the witch herself. And besides, Aileen knows the Morrigan; she would never fall for any of her tricks."

"The Shape-shifter is very clever," said Aggie shaking her head. "She knows just how to lure creatures and humans into her traps."

Robin's blood turned cold. If what Aggie said was true then Aileen was in dreadful danger.

"What should we do?" he asked.

"There is nothing we can do but watch," replied Aggie. "When the Morrigan calls on Aileen to do her bidding we must be ready. The call will come at night and I feel in my bones that it will be soon. I am old and need little sleep. I will keep watch tonight – but I may need your help."

Before going to bed, Aileen tidied away after the visitors and then went to say goodnight to her mother. She found her exhausted after the events of the day and Tom was going into the spare room so that she could have a good night's sleep. He wanted to take the baby with him but his wife would have none of it. After Tom left, Aileen went over to the cradle to look at the baby. It was Aileen's old cradle all rigged up for the new arrival. Her mother was pleased to see her looking at the baby.

"He's a right wee man isn't he?" she smiled. Aileen smiled back but the smile didn't light up her eyes.

"Funny," said her mother. "I know I'm tired, but all of a sudden I can't keep my eyes open."

And her eyelids drooped and she slipped off into a

deep, deep slumber. Aileen looked down at the baby. He too was sleeping peacefully. She reached out a finger and a little warm hand opened and curled tightly round it. A flash of heat burned for a second deep within her. Then it died leaving the splinter of ice unchanged. She pulled her hand away and went to her room.

From his bedroom window Robin sat staring at the Scroggy farm house as he sipped from a can of Coke. Aggie Scroggy's words had disturbed him and even though the old woman had said she would watch for the Morrigan, Robin didn't go to bed for he knew he wouldn't sleep. He sat on the window-sill, fully clothed and wrapped in an army sleeping bag. He would watch the house all night if need be. It was almost midnight and the long evening twilight had only now been swallowed up by true darkness. It was very cloudy so that Robin wasn't even aware that there was a full moon.

In his hand he had his powerful binoculars. They had belonged to his father and they were very special. They were equipped with night sights so that he was able to see every blade of grass and every leaf of every tree around the Scroggy house – just as if it were broad daylight. Nothing much had happened since he had taken up his watch. One by one the lights in the house had gone off until a solitary beam gleamed in Aggie's room at the gable end. Soon that light too disappeared – but Robin knew that the old woman was wide awake, listening and watching. He too waited and watched.

Robin gave a sudden jerk and the tin of Coke went tumbling onto the floor in a fountain of fizz. He looked at his watch. It was now two o'clock and his bones ached from his long vigil on the hard window-sill. He must have dozed off for at least fifteen minutes. Guiltily he raised the binoculars. The Scroggy house was still in darkness and nothing moved. Outside, the night was calm and dry. The sky had cleared and only a thin layer of low cloud clung to the hill tops. It was not enough to obscure the ghostly light of the full moon that hung over Cloughderg Mountain.

In her room Aggie Scroggy was battling valiantly against sleep. She was sitting in her chair near the window and her bedroom door was open slightly so that she could see any shadows moving on the landing. Sleep was wrapping her in a cosy cocoon and she longed to close her eyes. There is a spell at work here, she told herself as she struggled to keep awake. The Morrigan has spun a web of sleep over the house and everyone is caught in it.

Aggie began to whisper her multiplication tables to herself and when she had finished the lot she began again at the two-times. Still she felt the irresistible pull of drowsiness and she was almost dropping off when something cleared her brain and brought her wide awake. A dark shadow had passed her door.

Across the way, snuggled into his window seat, Robin Drake saw a shadow too. It was a small shadow and it slipped quietly from the darkness of the house into the moonlight. It appeared to be carrying a white bundle. The shadow crossed the yard into the lane and then disappeared between the rocks and low bushes of the hillside. The figure was dressed in dark clothes but, through his marvellous binoculars, Robin had seen clearly the pale face and the long fair hair. Aileen

Kennedy was night walking!

Quickly, but very quietly, Robin crept through the sleeping house and out into the yard. He ran down the lane and there he met Aggie dressed in a warm overcoat and staring up the hillside.

"She has gone!" she said in distress. "I followed her as far as here but I'm too slow. She's got away on me."

"I think I know where she's going," whispered Robin. "I know the way. We don't have to keep her in sight."

Aileen had taken the path to Cloughderg Mountain; the quick and easy path that led to the Nameless Place. Aileen moved swiftly over the rocky terrain, looking neither to her right nor left but staring upwards at the summit of the mountain. Up and up she toiled as if drawn by the magnet of the moon. She could see the great craggy outcrop that crowned the mountain and the Stone of the Curses that pointed at the stars. Another short climb and she was there.

Robin and Aggie hurried in her wake and soon they stood at the entrance to the Nameless Place. Quickly they slipped behind a rock, hoping that their incredulous gasps had not betrayed their presence. The old woman and the boy looked at each other. They could not believe the awful scene their own eyes had just witnessed.

∽ The Opening of the Evil Eye ∽

When they had had time to catch their breath, Aggie and Robin peered out from their refuge and looked again to make sure that their eyes, and the moonlight, were not playing tricks on them. The platform of rock that was the Nameless Place now formed a natural theatre floodlit by the full moon. The Stone of the Curses stood silhouetted against the sky and the table of stone slabs had been transformed into an altar. Four giant candles marked each corner and in the middle a large bowl glowed with fire. Beside the bowl, shining brightly in the flame light, lay the Brod of Bres.

A phalanx of warriors, with studded shields and crossed spears, stood in a semicircle round the altar. They were women warriors, all with jet black hair and heavy leather tunics. Sheathed swords were strapped to their waists. On each side of the altar stood two figures. One was tall and very thin and dressed in a black robe with a cowl pulled over its head. It stood in the shadows and seemed to be faceless. The other embraced the light and the glow of the candles enhanced her terrible beauty. She stood proudly, her perfect face lifted towards the candle power and the fire blaze. Her yellow eyes glittered in triumph. It was the Hell Hag herself – the Morrigan!

Aileen stood at the end of the altar table with her back to Robin and Aggie. The Morrigan glided forward and placed two taloned hands on the girl's frail shoulders; she then kissed her on the forehead. Aileen was still as a statue carved from the mountain rock. The Morrigan raised a hand and two of the warriors stepped forward. They walked towards Aileen and relieved her of the bundle that she still carried. They placed it on the table and then stood back. Aggie drew in a sharp breath and Robin looked closely at the bundle. He was almost sure he saw it move.

A warrior now placed a small vessel in the Morrigan's hands. She scooped something from it and threw it into the bowl of fire. The fire hissed and the flames spurted in blue tongues that leaped high into the velvety sky. Robin cowered behind his rock terrified that the light of the flames would seek him out and expose his presence.

The flames died down and a low hum, like the purr of a contented lioness, started in the ranks of the women warriors. The Morrigan began a sinuous dance around the altar table. It was a rhythmic, writhing dance and the Hag circled and rippled with all the grace of a deadly cobra. The warrior hum became a chant of strange words and it grew loud and fast and frantic. The Morrigan paused to feed the fire bowl again and then, in the leaping light, she increased the pace of her swirling until she was circling the altar in a blur of waving arms and whirling skirts.

Suddenly spears slammed against shields in a crashing thunderclap and the crazed dancer threw herself on the ground before the altar. An expectant hush now stilled the Nameless Place. The Morrigan lay inert. Aileen remained a statue. The warriors were frozen in rigid obedience and the dark hooded figure still haunted the shadows. Robin was sure that the thud of his heartbeat could be heard in the ominous silence.

In the eastern sky, behind the Stone of the Curses, a delicate golden glow appeared. In one swift, supple movement the Morrigan was on her feet creating the illusion of a mystical resurrection. With arms clasped across her chest she walked towards the sheer drop of the cliff and stopped when her long naked toes curled round the edge. She raised her pale arms to the stars, flung back her head to bathe her cold face in the moonlight, and from her throat came a wild cry – the howl of an animal claiming territory.

Acting on this signal the warriors began to chant again, beating their spears against their shields in a menacing rhythmic tempo. All faces were now turned towards the glow in the eastern sky and voice and rhythm combined to urge the rising sun out of the ocean and into the heavens. The air was electric with tension as the ceremony proceeded. These were creatures of the Dark, Children of the Moon, and in courting the Sun they were playing with fire. But they needed the power of the mighty orb to achieve their wicked ends.

Robin began to realise what was happening. This was a ceremony to open the Eye of Balor! Before his own eyes the Riddle of the Evil Eye was unravelling. The moon was full and soon the Midsummer sun would rise. The Brod of Bres was there on the altar and only one part of the puzzle was still unclear – the bit about new life's bud. In some way, Aileen was needed for the completion of the ceremony. It was for this that the Morrigan had brought her here.

Helplessly Robin watched as the tip of the sun appeared above the horizon and the chanting grew more feverish and frenzied. The great orb rose refreshed from cool eastern waters and soon it was riding free and low in the morning sky.

The warriors now turned from the sun and the Morrigan walked towards the altar. She lifted the tiny Brod, raised it to her black lips and kissed it. She held it cupped in both hands and raised it high above her head, first towards the Moon that presided over the mountain and then towards the new risen Sun. A wolfish howl now filled the air as the warriors urged their leader on. The Morrigan walked slowly towards the great rounded crag that formed the summit of the mountain. Raising herself on tiptoe she slotted the Brod into a niche in the rock.

At that moment the first rays of the rising sun funnelled through the hole in the Standing Stone, piercing it and turning it blood red. Now it really was the Red Stone of the Curses. The sunlight flooded through the stone forming a strong beam that illuminated the niche and its tiny occupant.

A terrified Robin saw the contours of an ugly and massive face appear in the great crag. In the centre of a broad forehead was a single closed Eye and at its corner was the niche with the Brod of Bres. The little two-faced carving shuddered and creaked as if it were being torn apart by a distant power and the huge rock, with its petrified face, trembled as if shaken by an earthquake. Particles of shattered rock crumbled and tumbled to litter the floor of the Nameless Place.

The shrill voice of the Morrigan crackled above the heaving of the mountain.

"The time is here," she screamed. "Come mortal slave, place the offering in the arms of the Lord of Death."

Mechanically, Aileen moved to the altar table and reached towards the white bundle. As she lifted it Robin heard a faint cry and he realised with horror that Aileen was holding the baby that was only a few hours old! From the gloom stepped the hooded spectre with arms stretched forth to receive the child. The arms were stripped bare of flesh and long, bony fingers clawed at the tiny bundle.

"Go now, Donn, Lord of Death," ordered the Morrigan. "Carry the new life across the ocean to the Island of the Dead. Make haste! The journey must be made whilst the light still pierces the Stone."

Donn, Lord of Death, raised the bundle that was the new-born baby and his cowl slipped back revealing a naked, grinning skull. The last part of the Riddle was falling into place – life's new bud was about to be borne away by Death!

Out over the Lough a cold mist began to swirl and thicken. It descended on the Nameless Place blotting out all but the beam of sunlight on the Brod of Bres. Thicker and thicker it grew until Robin could see only the outline of Donn, the Lord of Death. From out of the mist appeared a serpent's head, wide-mouthed and sharp-toothed. It reared high above the heads of the assembled audience. Robin looked up into the lifeless eyes and he realised that he was staring at the prow of a ship.

Gradually a black, ghostly galleon, manned by twelve hooded oarsmen, crept out of the mist. It hovered at the cliff edge of the platform, suspended on a sea of fog.

"Quickly," urged the Morrigan, "get on board and depart. Then the Mighty Eye of Balor shall open and all his boundless power will be mine. All the Worlds will be under my domain and I will bring war and destruction to the Otherworld and the Mortal World. Darkness will reign everywhere and my faithful slaves of the Underworld will emerge from the Weems and take possession of all."

Robin had almost forgotten about Aggie Scroggy who had witnessed the unfolding of the horror story in stunned silence.

"We have to do something," she now said tugging at Robin's sleeve.

"I know," he whispered. "But what? If they see us we won't last a minute. I wish there was someone here to help us."

"You are not alone, Robin."

The voice was familiar and very welcome. Robin turned to greet his friend but Lacklin placed a hairy hand across his mouth and pointed to the rocks around him. Many Firslav and Annalaire faces peeped from crevices and cracks and all were beautifully camouflaged against the mountain. Cathara and Allochar now stood beside Lacklin.

"We have been watching," whispered Allochar, "and we know what the Morrigan is doing. I fear this may be the end of our world."

"Can you do nothing?" asked Aggie.

"The Firslav have no magic," replied Lacklin sadly, "and so we are powerless against the Low Magic of the Morrigan."

"The Annalaire have some magic," said Cathara, "but it is not strong enough to stop the Morrigan. Only the High Magic of Mathgen, the Druid, is a match for the Three-Headed Hag."

"But where is he?" asked Robin. "Does he not know what is happening here?"

"The Children of Danu have gone to Inisfail, their beloved homeland. There they celebrate the great Festival of the Sun. They do not think there is any danger from the Morrigan at this time when the powers of the Light are strong and those of Darkness are at their weakest."

"Can you not summon them on your horns?" pleaded Robin.

"The distance is too great. They would not hear."

Out in the great arena of the Nameless Place the Lord of Death was climbing aboard the galleon and the women warriors were lining up to push the great prow out into the mist. The Morrigan stood with her back to the workers, her greedy eyes on the shivering Brod and the groaning Eye of Balor.

Robin rose to his feet but Lacklin pulled him back down.

"I can't just sit here watching," cried the boy.

"We can delay them if we attack," said Cathara.

"But we cannot stop them," added Allochar.

"It will mean certain death," said Lacklin.

Firslav looked at Annalaire and then nodded their heads solemnly.

"We are going to be her slaves anyway," said Allochar, "so we should not give in without a fight."

Swift telepathic messages seemed to pass through the ranks of the Firslav and Annalaire for, in the blink of an eye, horns were blasting and hundreds of arrows were winging their way towards the warriors of the Morrigan.

"Kill them!" screamed the Morrigan, angry at the unwelcome distraction, and the guard of women warriors advanced on their attackers wielding their savage swords. From a hundred Annalaire fingertips came skeins of silvery threads that wrapped the women and their deadly weapons in silken cobwebs.

All was confusion and mayhem and Robin and Aggie seized the opportunity to dash into the Nameless Place to look for Aileen. At first the flailing bodies of the warriors, as they struggled to cut themselves free from the sticky webs, obstructed their view but then they saw her. She was standing in a daze, oblivious to all that was going on around her. To Robin's surprise Aggie Scroggy tried to drag her towards the boat.

The black galleon of Death still floated on the mist. Standing under the dragon's figurehead was the Lord of Death, clutching his prize and waiting for the warriors to push him towards his evil destination.

"Go on, Aileen," urged Aggie. "You must do it!"

Aileen turned slowly and took a little step towards the boat.

"What are you doing?" asked Robin. "You can't make her get on the boat! He will take both of them."

Aggie ignored Robin and concentrated on Aileen.

"The baby had to be given willingly by one who shared his blood, Aileen," she said in an urgent voice. "That is why the Morrigan tricked you and made you her slave. The Lord of Death cannot possess the child until he has carried him to the Land of Death. Only the person who freely gave the child can take him back."

Aggie now gripped Aileen by the shoulders and began to propel her towards the boat.

"He is your brother, Aileen," she insisted. "You must save him!"

The old woman gave the girl a final thrust and she was now within reach of the deathly spectre and the white bundle. But Aileen would go no further. All Aggie's desperate pleading had no effect. Aileen stubbornly refused to budge another inch. She stood in passive silence like a soulless, human iceberg.

"Take your brother from the arms of Death, please, Aileen. I beg you!"

Aggie was worn out beseeching. "You try, Robin," she said.

Robin looked at Aileen's blank eyes.

"You must do as she says, Aileen," he said very slowly. "The Morrigan has tricked you. You are under her spell and you are helping her to open the Eye of Balor."

Aileen's eyes now began to swivel from Robin to Aggie and back again to Robin. Snatches of elusive memories flitted through her brain and her face showed the strain as she struggled to snare them.

"It's me, Robin Drake," shouted the boy as he grabbed Aileen's arms and shook her. "You must remember me. We're a team, you and me. Us against the Worlds! Do as Aggie says. Look at the baby! You have to save him!"

Aileen took a slow hesitant step towards the boat and her friends moved with her, hoping that their words had penetrated her shield of cold steel.

A scream that would have curdled a fresh mountain stream now rent the air. The Morrigan had seen what was happening! She rushed towards the intruders and thrust them aside with a violent blow of her fist.

"You will not succeed!" she screamed. "This earth child is my slave! Come, Aileen the Fair, help me send the boat on its journey."

Meekly Aileen obeyed the command of her evil mistress. A ferocious battle continued to rage in the Nameless Place but Robin and Aggie were hardly aware of it. Helplessly they stood and watched as Aileen and the Morrigan began to push the galleon of Death into the mist and towards the Island of the Dead.

Nothing now remained of the ship but the ugly head of the dragon and the lone figure of Donn, Lord of Death. One more push and the galleon would disappear forever. The mist curled round the black-cowled skeleton and crept up to envelop the little white bundle.

"Push!" screeched the Morrigan. "The ship *must* be on its way while the sun still pierces the Stone!"

Willingly, Aileen bent her back to send the ship into everlasting oblivion.

Gently the ship slid into the fog until the staring eyes of the dragon disappeared from sight. The Morrigan raised her arms in victory and her coarse voice sang out in gleeful jubilation.

"Look at the Brod!" she exulted.

The little two-faced carving was shaking violently in its niche and a great crack had appeared in the rock that sealed the Eye of Balor!

"Open your Eye, Mighty Balor!" screamed the demented Hag. "Send your power to me, the Morrigan – Queen of the Underworld!"

The Firslav and the Annalaire were putting up a good fight against the huge warriors but they knew they could not win. They had retreated to the crown of the great head of Balor where they struggled to keep a foothold on the quaking mountain. From their lofty position they reigned down showers of tiny arrows on the advancing enemy.

Aileen stood transfixed staring after the Ship of Death. From the depths of the murky mist that had just swallowed it came a mewing cry. Aileen seemed to stiffen and listen. The cry came again, soft and plaintive. The splinter of ice, buried deep in her soul, shivered and then evaporated in a rush of melting heat.

"No, Aileen! No!" screamed Aggie as the girl plunged recklessly into the mist. "It's too late!"

"Yes, it is too late!" laughed the Morrigan. "See, the Eye opens!"

A terrible rumble came from Balor's Head and the crack in the rock widened into an ugly gaping gash as the Eye began to open. A still hush filled the Nameless Place. Not a breath sighed; not a hair moved. All watched and waited for the Awful Power to be unleashed on unsuspecting worlds.

∾ The Revenge of the Gods ∾

From out of the purling mist stepped a wraith-like figure. It was pale and pitiful and stood forlornly clutching a bedraggled armful of damp rags.

"Aileen!" breathed Aggie Scroggy in disbelief.

Aileen sank to the ground totally exhausted.

"My brother," she said smiling in wonder at the tiny face and then she looked up at the tearful old woman. "Your grandson, Aggie," she said and she handed the baby over.

At that precise moment the sun slipped higher into the morning sky and the beam of light that pierced the Red Stone of the Curses, died. The little Brod of Bres ceased its rocking and settled quietly in its niche; the deafening tearing apart of the rock stopped and the gap began to close. The Morrigan sent an anguished howl of loss and frustration rattling against the mountain and she flung herself towards the closing Eye but it slammed shut with a resounding thud and she was left clawing the rock with her hooked talons.

"You have denied me victory!" she howled at Aileen. "Now you will pay! You will all pay," she threatened as she turned on the Firslav and the Annalaire. "My Fomar dwellers of the Underworld will claim revenge!"

The Morrigan's face quivered and shook and, in

rapid succession, changed from beautiful woman to hook-beaked crow and finally to fork-tongued serpent. Her body trembled and shimmered and glossy black feathers became smooth scaled reptile skin. She hissed and spat and bared her venomous fangs and the creatures of the Underworld crawled out of their holes to avenge their Queen.

From the Wentel Trap slid the Vilesvart vipers, from the swamps squelched the half-blind Slobbolg and, worst of all, out of the dark belly of the Weems came the Lucorban. They lurched along on their hairy legs, brandishing their lethal crab-claws that could slice through rock as easily as butter. Through the air flew rat-like winged creatures with needle teeth bared, ready to tear into soft flesh. The Morrigan had failed to gain control over all the worlds but she would wreak havoc on all who had stood in her path.

The children and Aggie Scroggy were soon surrounded by every vile creature that peopled the Underworld. Up in their lofty positions the Firslav and Annalaire were relieved that they had hindered the Morrigan's dreadful plan and now they prepared to face certain death.

Aileen's brain raced as she tried to find a way of escape. She couldn't remember how she came to be on Cloughderg Mountain but she knew that she was in some way responsible for the terrible situation they all now faced. Her eye fell on the little Brod of Bres as it sat quietly in its niche. The only people strong enough to do battle with the Fomar were the Children of Danu, and the only Magic powerful enough to challenge the Morrigan's was the High Magic of Mathgen, the Druid.

It was the Brod that had first brought Aileen and

Robin to Mathgen; maybe this time it could bring the Druid to them?

The Morrigan stood between Aileen and the Brod and if the she-serpent knew what the girl was going to do she would surely snatch the little statue out of her reach.

"Do something to attract the Morrigan's attention," Aileen whispered to Robin. "I'm going to get the Brod."

Robin looked at her, not understanding at first. Then he nodded in agreement.

Quickly the boy gathered an armful of stray Firslav arrows and then he darted towards the lizard-like creature that was the Morrigan. He darted under her scaly arms until he was right beneath her soft white underbelly. Then, with all the strength he could muster, he jabbed an arrow into the milky flesh. The Morrigan yelped and pulled out the offending thorn in her side. Robin darted and dodged, like the first-rate footballer that he was, and planted more and more arrows until the Morrigan was twisting and growling in torment.

Meanwhile, Aileen had made a mad dash to the frozen head of Balor and began to climb towards the niche. She grabbed the Brod. The little carving was badly cracked but still in one piece. She scrambled down off the rock face and ran to the edge of the rocky platform where she faced out over the sea. With her eyes tightly shut and using every pick of energy she could summon, she held the Brod tightly in both hands and raised it high above her head. Then she called out in a loud voice,

"Mathgen! We need your help! The Fomar will destroy us. Please, Mathgen, listen to me."

Out over the ocean spread the distant, fluting sound

of a hundred golden trumpets and panic broke out amongst the Fomar. Across the Lough, from the Stone House of the Sun, came a growing thunder of horses, hooves and soon over the waters and through the air came a magnificent army. Warriors on white steeds brandished swords that glinted in the sun. Long manes of hair, encircled with bands of gold, flowed over tunics of saffron, green and deep purple and drooping moustaches curled and fell towards brawny shoulders. Each magnificent warrior carried a shield of leather and bronze blazoned with swirling designs of circles within circles. The goddess Danu had summoned her slumbering army and they had left their chamber, deep under the hill of Grianan, to answer her call.

From the east, as if riding on the slanted rays of the morning sun, came a chariot drawn by four white horses prancing nimbly and gracefully through the air. In the chariot stood the most magnificent warrior of all. His face shone bright as the sun from whence he came and his hair was spun from purest gold. Bands of gold ringed his throat and head and the sword he held aloft was studded with jewels and threaded with delicate designs in gold and silver.

"Lugh!" gasped Aileen in amazement. "Lugh, the young god of the Sun!"

"And the Cathadbolg – the Sword of Fate," whispered Robin who now stood at her side.

Lacklin leaped from Balor's brow and came to join the children. All around them the Fomar were screaming in fright and fighting each other to escape into their holes.

"The Children of Danu are answering your call," he said to Aileen. "We must go now and leave *them* to

115

deal with the Fomar."

Beasts, vipers and clawed Lucorban were now tumbling over each other to escape from the wrath of the gods as the children and Aggie, holding on tightly to the still-sleeping baby, followed Lacklin. Before she left the Nameless Place, Aileen turned to have a last look. The Morrigan in her serpent shape had vanished but above the fleeing Fomar a hooded crow now circled.

Glad to be leaving the scene of their near-death they hurried down the slope that led to home. But their troubles were not over yet. On a rock overlooking a bend in their path stood a huge grey crow. In the blinking of an eye the crow changed into the beautiful but evil woman.

"I have lost this time," she spat, "and the blame is yours. There will be another time for me but not for you. Be prepared to spend eternity as slugs and slow-worms."

The hag changed again and from her shoulders sprouted her three heads – the serpent, the crow and the beautiful witch. She raised her sceptre and from the jewelled eyes of the serpent that adorned its head sizzled a blue light.

"Cease your wicked savagery!" shouted a welcome and familiar voice. Three pairs of yellow eyes looked with loathing at a spot behind the children.

"Mathgen!" the children shouted when they saw the flowing beard and the startling blue eyes of the Druid.

"Your time of Evil is over," said Mathgen to the cowering Morrigan. He stepped forward, raised his white Rod of High Magic and struck each monstrous head once. In a flash the Morrigan had vanished. In her place stood a pillar of mountain rock. Beside the rock grew a straggly whin bush with six yellow blossoms shining like angry eyes. On the branch of the bush sat a tiny wren, her tail cocked in surprise.

"It is finished," said Mathgen turning to the shocked mortals. "You may go in peace now."

"Is she really gone forever?" asked Aileen.

"Once before I asked you, 'What is forever?' My Magic is strong but not strong enough to destroy the Morrigan. She is cunning and will search for ways to break my spell. But you need have no fear. I have sealed her scorpion underlings into their caverns and pits and without their help the Morrigan cannot use what power she has."

The Firslav and the Annalaire were now saying goodbye to each other and preparing to leave for their own worlds.

"The Children of Danu and all the peoples of the Otherworld are indebted to you, my friends," said Mathgen. "We were not vigilant and the Morrigan almost succeeded in her evil plan. The Eye of Balor almost poured its torrent of filth into her grasping hands." A smile lit up the wrinkled face.

"The interference of mortals has saved the Otherworld. Human curiosity has won the day!"

Mathgen then told the children that it was time to say goodbye to all their friends from the Otherworld.

"Will we never see you nor the Firslav nor the Annalaire again?" asked Robin.

"Can we never again cross the Threshold into the Otherworld?" asked Aileen.

The Druid placed his hands on Aileen's shoulders and smiled at her.

"You would never have been able to cross the Threshold in the first place without the help of the Brod of Bres, Aileen the Fair," he said gently. "You must give it to me now for the Two-in-One still holds the balance of power between the Fomar and the Danu. It is not safe in Mortal hands."

Reluctantly Aileen held out her clenched fist and slowly she opened it. The little Brod of Bres lay cradled in her palm and then, very gracefully, it fell apart. It was no longer a Two-in-One. Two tiny faces stared up at her; one as beautiful as a spring morning and the other as ugly as sin.

"The Power has left it!" exclaimed the old Magician. "The Brod of Bres can no longer be used for wicked purposes. It will never open the Eye of Balor."

"Does that mean I can keep it?" asked Aileen.

"You found it in the first place," said Mathgen shrugging his shoulders. "So I think our Mother Danu must always have meant you to have it."

Aileen threw her arms around the old magician and hugged him until he managed to escape. Then she said farewell to Cathara and Allochar. Lastly she went to her Firslav friend, Lacklin, and again she flung her arms around the little goatman.

"I will never forget you," she snuffled into his hairy chest.

Robin and Aggie then said their goodbyes and the trio continued their journey to the bottom of the mountain. Once there they turned and looked back. The path was empty. Above them a dense mist cloaked the top of Cloughderg Mountain and the Red Stone of the Curses.

Aggie let them look for a while and then she hurried

them home. She was anxious to slip the baby back into his cradle before he was missed. She need not have worried. The occupants of the Scroggy house still lay wrapped in the arms of a charmed slumber.

∾ Onwards to Glory! ∾

Four days later the assembly hall in Drumenny School buzzed with excitement and busyness. It was the day of the judging of the Leavers' Projects. Most of the charts and pictures were already mounted along the walls and display tables were crowded with a great variety of exhibits. Last-minute finishing touches were added with glue and Sellotape and then, miraculously, all the projects were ready for inspection.

"It looks great, doesn't it?" said Robin stepping back to admire their handiwork. And indeed it did. The title – the Red Stone of the Curses – had been done for them in lovely Celtic script by Robin's grandfather and the children themselves had told the legend of Cloughderg Mountain in colourful strip cartoons. There was Corgenn carrying the slain body of the Dagda's son and there was the great battle between the Fomar beasts and the Children of Danu. Balor looked deliciously hideous with his one Eye and ugly face and Lugh, the Sun god, was magnificent as he raised the Caladbolg and turned the severed head of the giant into stone. It was all lovely and gory and really horrific.

"I think we stand a good chance," decided Aileen as

she looked around at the competition.

"That's what *you* think," came a sneering voice from over her shoulder.

"Who wants to know about stupid old fairy stories and monsters with daft names? That's for babies."

The voice belonged to Nuala Deery and she stood linked with her friend Lisa as they rubbished Aileen's and Robin's work.

"But Aileen's all into babies now, isn't she?" simpered Lisa in a baby voice. "She's got a little brother."

"Half-brother," corrected Nuala.

"Maybe she'll get the other half some day!" crowed Lisa and the two girls dissolved in gales of laughter at their own silly cleverness.

Aileen and Robin ignored them and concentrated on arranging their display table. It was laid out in a battle scene and they had made models of all the principal characters in the drama. Aileen was particularly proud of the Morrigan – it wasn't easy to get three heads on one pair of shoulders! Mathgen looked very dignified and he was surrounded by the vile crawlers and the creepers from the Underworld.

"Toys!" drooled Lisa McCarron in a superior tone. "Some people never grow up."

"Anyway," decided Nuala, "they haven't a hope. Ours will beat theirs rotten. Ours is brill."

Nuala was right – their project was brilliant. It was like a Hollywood production. The two girls had taken up more wall space than anybody else and four tables were needed for all their bits and pieces. They had done a survey on pollution in Lough Foyle and they had enough information to start up a Green Party all by themselves. They had diagrams and graphs of every description and loads of very impressive computer print-outs

"My daddy got me everything from work," boasted Lisa as she arranged a folding card of mounted photographs. The tables were littered with labelled water samples and statistics the length of your arm about fish numbers, effluent discharges, industrial waste, rubbish dumping and slurry flow from farms. It all looked very professional.

"It's the in thing now," continued Lisa, "the environment and all that. Beats stupid comic stories anyway."

All the classes in the school were being allowed to view the projects before the headmaster and the class teacher made their decisions. The younger pupils were all straining and pushing at the hall doors to get in. They weren't all that anxious to see the exhibition but anything is better than classwork.

"Stop that din along there!"

The headmaster's famous voice came rolling along the corridor echoing off the walls and silencing the assembled pupils.

"Get into a proper line there. We'll have a bit of order before I open these doors!"

Mrs McCloskey, the class teacher, hurried to the door to greet Mr Quinn and she was very nervous and twittery. The headmaster had great hopes of winning the competition for the publicity and prestige it would bring to the school and so he was bound to be looking for very high standards.

The doors were opened and the children began

milling around the stands; the Red Stone of the Curses proved very popular. They liked the cartoons and the models and the younger classes in particular were fascinated by the thought of the monster Balor being trapped in the rock at the top of Cloughderg Mountain. They asked loads of questions about the Riddle of the Evil Eye and their own eyes opened wide as Robin and Aileen explained what it meant. When they described the Morrigan and her evil slaves there was enthralled silence. Their descriptions were extremely good; one would almost have thought they were speaking from memory!

"Huh!" snorted Lisa McCarron. "What did I tell you? Kids' stuff!"

"I think you will find this very interesting, Mr Quinn," gushed Mrs Mac as she directed Lambeg towards Lisa and Nuala's project. This was obviously her favourite and she wanted to impress Lambeg. He *was* impressed too. He examined everything in detail and asked a lot of questions. The two girls swelled with pride and importance and did a terrible bit of showing off. They were rhyming off lists of facts and figures when the headmaster's attention began to wander. There seemed to be a bit of fun at one of the stands a few tables along and his curiosity was roused.

"Thank you very much, girls," he said halting Nuala's flow. "That all sounds very . . . ah . . . very . . . ah . . . scholarly." And he sidled away to where all the action was.

"Well now, what have we here?" he boomed in Aileen's ear.

She began to tell him and soon Lambeg was even

more absorbed in the story than the five-year-olds.

"This is marvellous!" he shouted all over the hall. "This is just the sort of thing I was looking for. It's a great story altogether. We have local history and colour and the whole thing is completely original and very well researched. What's this?" he asked poking at the Brod of Bres that lay in pride of place at the front of the table.

"It could be the Brod of Bres that is mentioned in the Riddle," suggested Aileen. "The statue that King Bres was turned into by the god Lugh."

Lambeg laughed a laugh that would have deafened a heavy metal fan.

"Oh, that's good," he chuckled. "I like to see the imagination at work. A bit of creative thinking lends spice to a good yarn. And how do you think it came to be broken?"

"Maybe it happened one time when the Morrigan tried to open the Evil Eye," suggested Robin.

"Great stuff!" beamed the headmaster nodding his head. "So, some time or other we were all in danger of being taken over by this three-headed demon and we didn't even know it? You're not safe in your bed these days are you?" he chuckled.

Lambeg spent some more time examining the old maps and books that Robin and Aileen had on display and listening to Aggie Scroggy on tape as she told a version of the story of Balor of the Evil Eye that she had heard as a child. Then he clapped his huge hands and addressed the gathered school.

"Right. Now, I think you have all seen everything so you will leave the hall in an orderly fashion and Mrs

McCloskey and I will remain behind to reach our decision."

The children began to file out but everyone knew which was the winning project. Mrs McCloskey knew too. There was no point in even discussing it with the headmaster. He had made his decision and she wouldn't get a vote at all. She sighed and pretended to listen to his ear-splitting enthusiasm.

Later the children were all gathered again in the hall and Robin and Aileen were given a standing ovation.

"You will go forward to the regional finals now," announced Mr Quinn, "and I have no doubt you will sweep the boards. There won't be another project fit to beat the Story of the Red Stone of the Curses. You'll be in *Áras an Uachtaráin* before the summer's out!"

"Humph!" said Lisa McCarron in a loud whisper. "Only if the other judges are as stupid as he is."

"He's just an overgrown wean," added her friend.

"Do you think we'll win?" asked Aileen as she and Robin sat in her favourite spot along the shores of Lough Foyle.

"You'd never know. Stranger things have happened," grinned Robin and Aileen found herself laughing along with him. She looked up at Cloughderg Mountain and its pointing finger. The Stone looked very innocent in the bright sunlight. She poked a finger at the baby as he slumbered peacefully in his carry-cot. Already his cheeks had filled out and his little chubby fingers had a strong grip on his bottle.

"Thomas Paul," said Aileen as she traced the outline of his bald head. She had amazed everybody, even herself, at how much she doted on her brother. It was the school holidays now and she rarely went anywhere without him.

"It's been a funny old year," she said thinking back on all that had happened since the start of the school year. "What do you think it will be like in our new school?"

"Peaceful, I hope," replied Robin. "Peaceful and quiet and very ordinary."

Also by Poolbeg

The Pit of the Hell Hag

By

Mary Regan

When Aileen Kennedy finds a tiny two-faced figurine, the Brod of Bres, on a deserted beach near her house, she and her best friend Robin Drake are drawn into the otherworld – a world which exists alongside our own. There they meet Mathgen, the chief Druid of the Tuatha De Danaan, and the evil sorceress, the Morrigan.

As Samhain, or Hallow E'en, draws near, the Morrigan's magic is at its strongest. She wants to steal the powerful Brod because it can be used to open the Eye of Balor, the source of all evil. Aileen and Robin join the weird and wonderful beings of Mathgen's world to battle against the vile creatures of the Morrigan's underworld.

When Aileen is taken prisoner in the Pit of the Hell Hag, the Morrigan has the Brod in her grasp. Will Robin be able to stop the Morrigan and save Aileen?

Also by Poolbeg

The Spirit of the Foyle

By

Mary Regan

When a hill collapses on a construction site at the Grianan of Aileach, an ancient historic site near Derry city, the Brod of Bres is once again uncovered. This little two-faced figurine has already involved Aileen Kennedy and her friend, Robin Drake, in dangerous encounters with the Morrigan, the dreaded Shape-shifter, eager to possess the mysterious powers of the Brod.

A school visit to the Tower Museum allows the children to see the Brod on display, but they also encounter an old enemy and suspect that the Morrigan has plans to steal the Brod.

Caught up in a dangerous web of intrigue the children must use all their ingenuity to outwit the power-hungry Morrigan.

Also by Poolbeg

Shiver!

*Discover the identity of the disembodied voice singing
haunting tunes in the attic of a long abandoned house . . .*

*Read about Lady Margaret de Deauville who
was murdered in 1814 and discover the
curse of her magic ring . . .*

*Who is the ghoulish knight who clambers out of his tomb
unleashing disease and darkness upon the world?*

*Witness a family driven quietly insane by an evil
presence in their new house . . .*

*What became of the hideous voodoo doll
which disappeared after Niamh flung it from
her bedroom window?*

An atmospheric and suspense-filled collection of
ghostly tales by fifteen of Ireland's most popular
writers: Rose Doyle, Michael Scott, Jane Mitchell,
Michael Mullen, Morgan Llywelyn, Gretta Mulrooney,
Michael Carroll, Carolyn Swift, Mary Regan, Gordon
Snell, Mary Beckett, Eileen Dunlop, Maeve Friel,
Gaby Ross and Cormac MacRaois.

Each tale draws you into a web at times menacing,
at times refreshingly funny.

Also by Poolbeg

The Secret of Yellow Island

By

Mary Regan

*The Spirits of the past have risen at
last to do battle with the spirit that is
ageless – the spirit of evil.*

When Eimear Kelly arrives in Donegal to
spend the summer with her eccentric granny,
Nan Sweeney, she is not prepared for the
adventure about to unfold.

Who is the frightening giant of a man Eimear
christens 'the Black Diver' who has rented her
gran's holiday cottage? What is his dark secret
and why is he poking about the deserted
island of Inishbwee?

When Eimear meets Ban Nolan, a mysterious
old woman, and discovers the legend of the
Spanish sea captain, she is drawn into many
exciting and dangerous encounters.

The Secret of Yellow Island is a story of a
strange and unforgettable summer holiday.